DOCTOR WHO
DRAGONFIRE

Based on the BBC television series by Ian Briggs by
arrangement with BBC Books, a division of BBC
Enterprises Ltd

IAN BRIGGS

Number 137 in the
Target Doctor Who Library

A TARGET BOOK
published by
the Paperback Division of
W.H. ALLEN & Co. Plc

A Target Book
Published in 1989
By the Paperback Division of
W.H. Allen & Co Plc
Sekforde House, 175/9 St. John Street,
London, EC1V 4JY

The BBC producer of *Dragonfire* was John Nathan-Turner
The director was Chris Clough
The role of the Doctor was played by Sylvester McCoy

Printed and bound in Great Britain by
Cox & Wyman Ltd, Reading

ISBN 0 426 20322 4

With grateful thanks to John Nathan-Turner for his helpful
comments and suggestions on the original scripts, and
particularly to Andrew Cartmel, *il miglior fabbro*.
Thanks also to the children and teenagers in Ealing who
inspired it – particularly Annamarie, Joanne and Juno.

CHAPTER ONE

Sergeant Kracauer's words hung mockingly in the frosty air of the Cryogenics Chamber.

'Oh you lucky, *lucky* people . . .' He paced in front of the new volunteers, eyeing them suspiciously. Six thugs – four men, two women – with more muscle than brain, recently the crew of the space-vessel *Nosferatu*. '*You* are the chosen ones,' he taunted. 'The élite. Specially selected to join our crack band of mercenaries, to create fear and terror wherever you go.' He gestured round the dark chamber at row upon row of vertical tubes – over a hundred of them, maybe a thousand. The tubes, mostly opaque with frost, contained the motionless figures of humans caught frozen in suspended animation.

Kracauer halted in front of one of the new recruits and stared at him. A grimy, rough-faced crewman whom Kracauer had marked down as a troublemaker as soon as he saw him. The rough-faced man snarled back defiantly, 'We were tricked!'

Kracauer smiled. 'Mr Kane paid seventeen crowns for each of you – and Mr Kane always insists on getting his money's worth.'

'Seventeen crowns?' The rough-faced man's eyes began to blaze with anger. 'You couldn't buy a *dog* for seventeen crowns.'

In a single, powerful movement, Kracauer grabbed the man, and dragged him forward. The sergeant's voice was no longer mocking. It was full of threat. '*Precisely. I* wouldn't have paid seventeen crowns for the lot of you, let alone each.' He saw the fear in the man's face, and laughed, releasing his victim with a slight push. The rough-faced man fell back, and clutched at an open-topped vat steaming with low temperature gases. His face contorted with pain as he felt the biting cold burning into the flesh of his hand.

Kracauer laughed again. 'Only frost-burn,' he mocked. 'The vats contain liquid nitrogen at minus 200 °C. Just be grateful your arm didn't go *inside* the vat – otherwise it wouldn't have come out again . . .' He turned to one of the two guards standing over the new recruits. 'Right, freeze them!' he ordered crisply.

The crewmen and women began to shuffle fearfully. A dark-haired crew-woman – either braver or more foolish than the others – spoke up. 'You mean we're going to be frozen?'

Kracauer turned to her. 'Until Kane needs your services, yes. What's the matter – getting cold feet?' He laughed at his little joke.

The rough-faced crewman looked round quickly. There were only two guards. One was preparing the six cryogenics tubes that stood waiting for the new volunteers. The other was momentarily occupied as he pushed the dark-haired woman back into line. The crewman took his chance. He threw himself on the nearest guard and wrestled the gun out of his hands. He then fired off several shots before the second guard could reach for her own gun. The pulse beams cut through the air in a series of random lines. Everyone but Kracauer dropped to the ground for safety. One of the cryogenics tubes exploded as an aimless pulse beam burst into it like a detonator.

The rough-faced man looked round for an escape route. They had been marched into the Cryogenics Chamber through a doorway beside the equipment

6

controls. But even if he could get past the guard who was now turning her gun on him, he would encounter more guards down the passageway, drawn by the sound of weapons firing. As the guard pulled her gun up into a firing position, the man spun round and took the only alternative: a bulkhead doorway marked *Restricted Zone*. He hauled on the door as the guard's first shot exploded against the wall alongside. Sheer terror gave him a strength he had never known before. He felt the guard's second shot graze his shoulder, and burning metal sparks from the door showered his face. The guard's third shot came too late and exploded into an empty doorway, through which the rough-faced man had escaped barely a moment earlier.

The guard turned to Kracauer for orders. Kracauer smiled. 'Leave him. He's in the Restricted Zone. He's a dead man . . .'

Whatever the crewman might have expected to find through the door to the Restricted Zone, he was completely unprepared for the chill gloom he now found himself in. Huge, shadowy walls of ice intersected at right-angles, turning the huge chamber into a confusing maze. Ice boulders lay at the foot of the walls, and the crewman had to pick his way carefully. As in the Cryogenics Chamber, vats of supercooled gases overflowed with a silent mist. Far away, he heard a thundering echo that sounded like icebergs shearing away from one another – except there was no sea here on the planet Svartos. Closer by, he heard the shimmering tinkle of icicles. And, faintly but insistently, there was a tapping sound.

The crewman moved nervously among the boulders of ice and the mist-shrouded vats. As he picked his way through the ice and moved deeper into the Restricted Zone, the tapping sound grew louder. He followed the sound.

As he grew closer to the source of the sound, the Restricted Zone seemed lighter, allowing the man to make out detail in the shadows of the ice walls. He edged nervously towards the light and the strange tapping sound, which seemed to be coming from behind an ice wall in front of him. He readied his gun, tensed himself, and suddenly threw himself round the corner into the light, with his gun levelled at the source of the sound – whatever, or whoever, it might be.

His eyes opened wide in amazement.

He saw a brightly lit clearing amongst the ice walls and boulders. In the middle of the clearing stood a huge, rectangular block of clear ice. Beside it, a man wearing a sculptor's smock was chipping at the ice with a hammer and chisel.

The Sculptor stopped, and turned to look at the gun pointing at him. He seemed more puzzled than frightened.

The crewman was startled and confused by the Sculptor with his block of ice. He suspected some kind of trap, and wheeled round with his gun, in case someone should creep up behind him. But there was no one there. Just a large horizontal cabinet standing empty nearby, looking like a coffin with a clear lid.

The crewman wheeled back towards the Sculptor. As he did so, he slipped on the ice and fell sideways. The gun fell from his hand, and tumbled into one of the vats of supercooled gases. He tried to grab at it as it bounced on the rim of the vat, but he was too late. He saw it disappear into the frozen mist.

Carefully, he tried to reach into the freezing gas to retrieve the weapon. He reached into the cold mist, but as his hand came within a few centimetres of the liquid gas, he felt the biting cold eat into his flesh like acid. Instinctively, he pulled his arm away. He tried again, thinking of the gun that might save his life, but again the pain was too much. He crouched over the vat, nerving himself for another attempt. Suddenly another arm plunged deep into the vat of agonising cold.

The crewman watched in horror as the stranger's arm pulled the gun out of the liquid gas. The flesh of the stranger's hand was now caked in hard, dry frost. The crewman looked up. The stranger was dressed in the same clinical white uniform of the Iceworld guards, but where the others bore an official name patch on the chest of their uniform, the stranger's said simply KANE. The crewman looked up at Kane's face. It was deathly pale, apart from the intense shiny black of Kane's eyes. There was no emotion in the face.

Kane held the gun out for the crewman to take. Mesmerised, the crewman took the gun. He instantly felt the biting cold of the superfrozen weapon, and dropped it with a cry of pain. The gun hit the ground and shattered into fragments. A slight smile seemed to flick across Kane's face, but quickly disappeared. Without taking his piercing black eyes off the crewman, Kane carefully removed the white glove from his other hand. The crewman watched, like an animal hypnotised by a cobra. Kane slowly reached forward as if to embrace the crewman's face. He pressed his hands against the man's flesh. Immediately, the crewman felt the frozen cold eating into his skull. He struggled briefly against the searing pain, but quickly fell unconscious. Kane held on until he felt the last spark of life die in the crewman, and then released him. The crewman fell to the ground. The prints of Kane's hands were branded on the crewman's face.

Kane turned to the Sculptor, who had been watching quietly. He spoke softly to the Sculptor, 'Pay no attention to the intruder. You may return to your work.' Obediently, like a faithful servant, the Sculptor turned back to his block of ice and resumed his task.

CHAPTER TWO

The Doctor looked at Mel's inverted face. She was balanced in a headstand against one of the walls in the TARDIS Console Room. Her face looked peaceful, but it had a sort of ... well – an upside-down quality about it. She hadn't moved for the last twenty minutes. The Doctor looked slightly crestfallen – like a child who's lost his playmate. He turned to the viewing screen showing the clear image of a planet. He turned back to Mel and cleared his throat loudly. There was no response from Mel.

'Mel?'

Still no response. 'Can I tempt you to a jelly baby? You can have the red ones ...'

Again no response. *She can't be dead*, he thought, *otherwise she'd have fallen over*. He sighed. There was nothing else for it. He pushed at a slide control on the central console. The background hum of the TARDIS suddenly grew louder and the time machine lurched drunkenly.

There was a thud and shriek from behind the Doctor.

'Ah, Mel,' he said brightly, turning to the heap on the floor, 'back in the Land of the Living at last.' The heap on the floor, however, was in no mood for such good humour.

'Doctor!' it screeched. 'You did that deliberately!' Mel picked herself off the floor, and began to advance on

10

the Doctor.

'What, me?' protested the Doctor, backing away slightly, and wondering if overloading the TARDIS's stabiliser circuit had been such a phenomenally good idea after all.

'I was meditating! I was in a state of blissful serenity!'

The Doctor didn't know much about states of blissful serenity, and he continued to play the innocent. 'No, honest, Mel – temporary fluctuations in the ion field ...'

'I'll give you temporary fluctuations!'

The Doctor wasn't too sure what Mel had in mind, but it sounded unpleasant. He'd never had an older sister, but he was beginning to understand why they had such a bad reputation. He decided a different approach was called for. He pointed to the viewing screen. 'Look – the planet Svartos.'

Mel peered at the screen. One side of the planet was baked in the intense heat from the nearby sun, but the dark side was cold and mysterious. A large structure which appeared to be made out of gigantic ice crystals glistened on the dark surface. And Mel could just make out several tiny spacecraft, which were either just approaching or just leaving the outer crystalline limbs. 'What's that on the dark side?' she asked, turning to the Doctor.

'That's Iceworld – a Space Trading Colony. Space travellers stop here for supplies.' He turned excitedly to Mel. 'I've been picking up some faint tracking signals. I'm sure there's something interesting going on!'

Mel's face broke into a broad smile. It was no use trying to be angry with the Doctor – not when there was always another adventure waiting just round the corner ...

The Freezer Centre was the size of a vast, low-ceilinged flight hangar. Brightly lit freezer chests stretched away as far as you could see, as hundreds of curious-looking

11

space travellers trundled their shopping trolleys up and down the aisles. Posters hanging over the freezer chests proclaimed various special offers: *Iceworld Free-Range Phoenix Eggs – 19:95 crowns per megagram, Iceworld Special Offer – Crab Nebula Pasties – now only 9:95 crowns per thousand.* Concealed loudspeakers waltzed with a forgettable melody that had been 'bubbling under' the Easy Listening charts here in the Ninth Galaxy for the last 200 years. The music was occasionally interrupted by a *bing-bong* as some cheery woman with a sing-song voice intoned a distant announcement: 'Don't miss our latest special offer in the Motoring Spares Department – photon refrigeration units for only 24:95. Thank you.' *Bing-bong*.

Stellar was fed up. She was a Starchild, looking roughly similar to a six-year-old Earth girl, and she was fed up of traipsing round a boring freezer centre with her mother. 'Do keep up, Stellar,' complained her mother from behind the mass of exotic black feathers that decorated her clothing. This mass of black feathers then turned to inspect the contents of another freezer chest, while Stellar trudged wearily behind wondering if they sold toys here.

There was a faint grinding sound coming from somewhere. Stellar looked round.

The sound was getting louder, but no one else appeared to have noticed it. It sounded like some kind of very old machinery, and it seemed to be coming from a gap between two freezer chests. As Stellar watched, she saw the faint outline of a tall object beginning to appear out of nowhere. She tugged at her mother's sleeve.

'Yes, darling – won't be a minute,' replied her mother, not bothering to emerge from the feathers.

The mechanical sound grew louder as the mysterious object materialised. There was a flashing blue light on top of the object, which stopped at the same time as the sound, once the object had fully materialised. Stellar had

12

never seen anything like this before. She tugged at her mother's sleeve once again.

'What is it, Stellar?' demanded her mother irritably, as she turned to see what her daughter was so concerned about. She looked at the tall blue cubicle now standing between two freezer chests. 'Yes, it's a Police Box, darling. They have them on a dirty planet called Earth. I'll show you some pictures when we get back to the spacecraft. Now where do you suppose they keep the deep-frozen lavatory paper ... ?' She flounced off down the aisle, pushing her trolley in front of her, and dragging her wide-eyed daughter behind her.

The Doctor emerged cautiously from the TARDIS and looked round. No one seemed to have noticed the TARDIS's arrival. He was constantly surprised at how people are so preoccupied with themselves that they never notice what's going on about them. Mel followed him out, and looked round.

'A freezer centre!' she exclaimed in dismay. 'I thought this was going to be an adventure!'

'Trust not to appearances, Mel. There's no knowing what kind of evil might be lurking in the freezer chests ... Follow me.'

The Doctor loped off towards a door marked *Refreshment Bar*, leaving the sensible-minded Mel wondering which was barmier – the Doctor, or the idea of a freezer centre in space – as she hurried after him.

Walk into a refreshment bar on any planet in the Twelve Galaxies and you might just as well walk into a refreshment bar on any of the other thousands of planets. They're all much the same. The same brightly coloured lighting and exotic fruit drinks everywhere. The same frontier-post bustle, with curious aliens arguing in strange languages. And the same bad-tempered barmen, who would rather spend their time polishing glasses and tumblers than serving customers.

In Iceworld, the barman was called Eisenstein, and he was currently glowering at three customers seated at the door. His assistant, a rebellious-looking sixteen-year-old waitress, was hurrying backwards and forwards with trayfuls of drinks. The three objects of Eisenstein's ill humour were a tall reptilian creature, a woman with blue hair and silver skin, and a small furry creature with disgusting table manners, who was actually a Galactic Ambassador. The woman seemed to be calling the Ambassador 'Erick' as she dropped small pieces of food into its mouth. Erick was managing to drool half of the food all over the table (which Eisenstein would have to clean up afterwards) and spit the rest of it over the customers sitting nearby. *Disgusting!* thought Eisenstein, as he watched a small piece of half-chewed seaweed fly out of Erick's mouth and arc gracefully down the cleavage of a pig-featured hologram model sitting three tables away. *Absolutely disgusting!*

Just then, the door swung open and the Doctor marched in, propelling Mel alongside him. He looked round, then straightened himself, and strode up to Eisenstein. 'Hello. We've just arrived. What can you recommend to quench the thirst and fortify the spirits, eh?'

'May I suggest an Astral Cascade, made with fresh orchid juice?' offered Eisenstein, grateful that the new customers at least seemed to have decent table manners. 'Completely non-alcoholic for zero-gravity travel, but it packs a punch like nitro-9!'

'Splendid! Just the thing. We'll have two of them, please.'

'Certainly, sir.'

At a table in a dark corner, another customer was arguing with the waitress. He spoke with a distinctive thick voice. 'There must be some mistake with the reckoning, Sprog...'

'The mistake's in your wallet, not my arithmetic!'

14

argued the teenage waitress back. 'And don't try and pay in Nebulous Shillings neither. I got into trouble for accepting them yesterday.'

The Doctor looked at Mel. There was something familiar about the customer's voice.

'Do you take Asteroid Express?' enquired the customer.

Of course!

'Glitz!' exclaimed the Doctor and Mel simultaneously, as they bounded across to the dark corner. Glitz choked on his milkshake.

'What? No. Never heard of him,' he replied, trying to hide his face.

'Of course it's you,' countered Mel. 'Don't you remember us – Mel and the Doctor? You haven't forgotten, have you?'

Glitz looked up. There was no mistaking the biggest rogue this side of the Greater Space Lanes: the rugged leather jerkin (for keeping out the astral storms), the securely tied money pouch (for containing the profits from his dubious financial deals), the neatly trimmed beard (for attracting the ladies), and the look of hurt innocence (for getting him out of trouble) – a rogue right down to the space dust on his boots. 'Shh! Keep your voice down!' he hissed.

He peered at Mel, trying to remember where he'd seen her before. 'Of course I haven't forgotten you ... er ...' Suddenly, he remembered. 'Mel! And the Doctor!' He turned to the Doctor to shake his hand, but instead of the Doctor he remembered from their last adventure together, he now saw a goon grinning like an idiot.

'Here – hold the space race ...' muttered Glitz suspiciously, 'you're not the Doctor.'

The Doctor turned away crossly. 'I've regenerated. The difference is purely perceptual.'

'Oh ... right ...' Glitz didn't have the faintest idea what the Doctor was talking about, but he knew from

15

experience that with the Doctor anything could happen. And it was a rule of Glitz's never to ask too many questions. The waitress, meanwhile, was getting restless.

'Here – what about this bill that you haven't paid?'

Glitz turned back to the Doctor. 'You couldn't help me out, could you, Doctor?' he whispered. 'Only – I appear to be temporarily financially embarrassed.'

The Doctor sighed, and pulled a handful of banknotes out of his pocket. He selected a ten crown note and gave it to Glitz. 'This is just a *loan*, you understand.'

'You're a gent.' Glitz passed the note to the waitress. 'Here you are – and I'll pay for my two friends as well. And keep the change.' The waitress's eyes opened wide in amazement. So did the Doctor's.

'Just a moment – that's a ten crown note!' But the waitress was gone.

Glitz leaned across to the Doctor. 'Here – you couldn't do me another favour, could you? You see, I'm in a spot of bother.'

'What is it this time, Glitz? Another dodgy deal of yours backfired?'

'No, nothing like that – straight up. Fact is ...' he glanced round, and then beckoned the Doctor and Mel to lean closer as he whispered, 'I'm on a mission of a highly philanthropic nature.'

'What's that?' whispered Mel.

Glitz looked at Mel. 'It means it's beneficial to mankind.'

'I know what *philanthropic* means! What's the *mission*?'

'I have been entrusted with the delivery of certain secret documents, which unnamed nefarious parties would stop at nothing to grasp within their own grubby digits.'

The Doctor looked at Glitz in horror. 'You mean ... they'd ...'

'... kill you?' continued Mel.

16

Suddenly, a hand fell on Glitz's shoulder. The Doctor, Mel and Glitz looked up to find themselves surrounded by guns. Captain Belázs had her hand on Glitz, holding him firmly in his place. 'Sabalom Glitz. We've been looking for you...'

Mel sprang up. 'Leave him alone! If you kill him, you'll have to kill us too!'

'Steady on, now, Mel...' cautioned the Doctor, watching the guns.

Captain Belázs turned to Mel in surprise. 'What *are* you talking about?'

'He's told us everything. About how you want to stop him delivering his secret documents.'

'Shh...' interrupted Glitz.

Belázs turned to Glitz, who was trying to smile innocently. 'Becoming quite a story-teller, aren't we, Glitz?' She turned back to Mel. 'The truth is, I'm not interested in any secret documents which Mr Glitz may or may not possess.' Mel and the Doctor looked at Glitz accusingly. His innocent smile was starting to wear thin. Belázs continued. 'I'm more concerned with the one hundred crowns he took from my employer, Mr Kane, under false pretences.'

'That was highest quality merchandise!' protested Glitz.

Belázs turned on him. 'It was a space-freighterful of deep-frozen fruit which turned out to be *rotten!*'

'A bit on the ripe side, maybe...'

'They were putrefying, Glitz!'

'A little past their prime, possibly...'

'And Mr Kane does not run Iceworld to subsidise crooks like yourself. The 100 crowns, please.' Belázs held out her hand for the money. Glitz looked to the Doctor for help, but the Doctor's goodwill had run out.

'I think you'd better return the money, Glitz.'

'I can't.'

'Why not?'

'Well, there was this game of cards... I got well damaged...'

'What about the 102 crowns you also sold your crew for?' interrupted Belázs.

Mel was appalled. 'Sold your crew?'

'The mutinous rabble!' retorted Glitz. 'The ungrateful cretins! I generously offered them ten per cent of the profits on our last deal, to share between them, and what did they do? Tried to take control of the spacecraft. But I was too smart for them, and they got well spanked! I relieved myself of them for seventeen crowns each – which was rather more than they were worth, I fancy!' Glitz chuckled to himself.

Belázs held out her hand. 'The money...'

Glitz smiled weakly at her. 'Gone the way of all organic matter, I'm afraid – down the tubes...'

'In that case, we're confiscating your spacecraft.'

'The *Nosferatu*? You can't do that!'

'Oh yes we can – unless you return the money you owe. You have seventy-two hours to find the 100 crowns, or you lose the spacecraft.' Belázs clicked her fingers at the other guards, who followed her as she walked smartly out. Glitz turned to the Doctor again.

'You've got to help me, Doctor.'

'You've only yourself to blame,' snapped the Doctor crossly. Glitz turned to Mel.

'Mel – think of the adventures we had together...'

But all Mel could remember was how she'd just been made to look an idiot by Glitz's scheming. 'You lied to us, Glitz.'

The Doctor and Mel both stood up and moved to a different table, where they struck up an interesting conversation with a pig-featured hologram model who'd just caused a diplomatic incident by stuffing a Galactic Ambassador into a plate of stewed seaweed.

CHAPTER THREE

In the Cryogenics Chamber, Sergeant Kracauer looked on as a clear tube descended over the immobile form of the dark-haired crew-woman. The four tubes next to her encased the other four members of the *Nosferatu* crew, and were already coated with a frosting of ice.

The door from the Restricted Zone hissed open, and Kracauer turned to see Kane enter the chamber. 'You're going to have trouble with this lot when you defrost them, Mr Kane.'

'Trouble?'

'They didn't volunteer willingly.'

'Ah ... *willingly* ...' Kane's black button-eyes scanned the rows of glistening tubes, each containing a motionless figure. 'But none of my mercenary force will be *willing* when I bring them out of cryo-sleep. Neither *willing* nor *unwilling*. The process causes complete loss of memory. With no memories, they can have no past, no future, no will of their own. No purpose except to obey me.' His eyes filled with cruelty, and his voice dropped to an evil whisper, 'My power shall be *absolute*.'

In the Refreshment Bar, the Doctor and Mel were now sitting by themselves, since the pig-featured hologram model had been rescued by her manager before she could cause any more diplomatic incidents with items from the menu. Glitz was sitting by himself, in disgrace, at an adjoining table. By the bar, the teenage waitress was arguing with Eisenstein. She was glaring angrily at a fatuous-looking couple at one of the tables. 'It's not my fault!' she protested. 'First they asked for two Vanilla Venuses – then one Vanilla Venus and one Starfruit Juice – and then two Starfruit Juices. How was I supposed to know that the bimbo had changed her mind again?'

'And we'll have less of your insolence, young lady.'

'I'm not telepathic,' grumbled Ace.

'You will do as you are told,' ordered Eisenstein. 'Now less of your lip, or you're out on your ear.'

'Yes, Mr Eisenstein.' Ace knew that she was beaten, and she couldn't afford to lose the job. She picked up the two Astral Cascades which the Doctor and Mel had ordered, and was still grumbling when she reached their table. 'If I didn't need the money, I'd chuck this job.' She plonked the drinks down, and then sat down herself. 'I hope he meets the dragon in a dark passage one night!'

'Dragon? What dragon?' asked Mel, mystified.

The waitress looked up as though she'd just noticed Mel for the first time. 'Oh, it's just some legend. There's supposed to be a terrifying dragon living in the Ice Passages beneath Iceworld. But I think the real dragon around here is Mr Eisenstein.'

Mel smiled broadly, and turned to the Doctor. 'Now I get it. I knew there must be a reason why you brought us here. You want to see a dragon, don't you?'

The Doctor was now bursting with enthusiasm. 'No, really, Mel – it's fascinating! Lots of people claim to have seen it over the centuries, but there's never been any proof, see?'

'You mean like the Loch Ness monster?'

'Lo*ch*...' corrected the Doctor with the authentic Scottish accent he'd acquired during his last regeneration.

The waitress was listening to this with growing disbelief. 'You're going to go looking for the dragon?'

'Absolutely!' affirmed the Doctor.

'Nah – it's just tinsel, innit?'

'Well, that's the whole point, young woman! If we were to go searching after an everyday coelacanth or dodo, it wouldn't be half as exciting!'

'What – you're really going to do it?'

'Scientific progress depends on it.'

'Cor – can I come too?'

The Doctor glanced over to Eisenstein. 'Are you sure you won't get into trouble with your boss?'

'Aw – I'm fed up of being a waitress. Go on, Professor – let me come too.' The Doctor looked at the waitress. She seemed bright and lively. A bit argumentative, maybe – but that's what teenagers were supposed to be.

'All right – join the party!'

The waitress almost jumped in the air. 'Ace! And can we search for the treasure too?'

This question took the Doctor by surprise. 'Treasure?'

'Yeah – the dragon's supposed to be guarding a fabulous treasure.'

At the next table, Glitz's ears pricked up at the mention of the word treasure. 'Treasure? What treasure?' He leaned across to the Doctor. 'You don't want to go believing in myths and legends, Doctor.'

'Who asked you?' retorted Mel. 'We're not talking to you – remember?'

Glitz ignored Mel. 'No, if you want my opinion, Doctor, this talk of dragons and treasure, it's all a load of space dust.'

'Well, if you're so convinced it's all rubbish,' began the waitress, leaning towards Glitz, 'why have you been burning holes in the treasure map for the last two days?' She suddenly snatched at an old document, tucked in Glitz's belt, and brandished it in the air above her head.

'Here – give us that back!'

Kane stood in his Control Room. The crystalline

21

structure of the room housed controls and display screens. Some of these were currently providing information about the running of Iceworld, but most of the displays were dark and empty. Kane stood silently.

One of the doors hissed open, and Belázs entered to report on her encounter with Glitz in the Refreshment Bar. Kane didn't move. Belázs waited, wondering if he hadn't heard her come in. Then he turned to her. 'Yes?'

'He says he lost the money in a game of cards.'

Kane narrowed his eyes to look at her. 'I *know* he lost the money in a game of cards. The game was fixed. Sabalom Glitz could never resist an easy opportunity to make money.'

'I gave him seventy-two hours in which to find the 100 crowns, or we take his spacecraft.'

'And the map?'

'He's convinced it's genuine.'

'Excellent. He'll soon realise that if he wants to see his spacecraft again, he has no alternative but to go after the treasure. And when he does, I'll be following him – every step of the way.'

'There's just one thing, Mr Kane.'

'Yes?'

'He appears to have two colleagues.'

'Colleagues? I thought you said he sold his entire crew?' Kane turned his piercing black eyes on Belázs. She suddenly felt as though two invisible laser beams were cutting into her mind and reading her thoughts.

'They're not from his crew. I made enquiries – they're space travellers, a girl and a man. Do you want them eliminated?'

Kane turned away and considered the suggestion. 'Not for the moment, I think. After all, there's no reason for these travellers to suspect that the seal on the map contains a radio tracking device.'

'As you wish.'

'They may even help Glitz find the treasure more

speedily. And once *they* have located the treasure, I shall follow the tracking device to locate *them*.'

Belázs thought she saw a momentary smile in his eyes.

At the table in the Refreshment Bar, Glitz's map did indeed look perfectly authentic, with its large, red wax seal in one corner of the old parchment. The Doctor had spread the map out and was examining it, while Glitz looked on anxiously.

'Fascinating,' murmured the Doctor. 'Absolutely fascinating.'

Mel was slightly more sceptical. 'You don't want to believe anything you get from Glitz, Doctor. He probably bought 200 of them in a job lot.'

Glitz bristled indignantly. 'Here – there's nothing snide about this document.'

'It looks like something from a jumble sale,' observed the waitress.

Glitz turned to her. 'Do you mind? This is the genuine oyster, this is. It comes from an unimpeachable source.'

'What's that, then?' demanded the waitress.

Glitz looked at her, slightly puzzled. 'It's something that's beyond reproach or question.'

The waitress glared at him. 'I know what *unimpeachable* means, Birdbath! But what makes you so certain that this map's pedigree is 24-carat?'

'Because I acquired it from a man of character and distinction.'

'How?'

'I won it in a . . .' Glitz suddenly realised that Mel was looking at him. '. . . in a . . . chess match . . .' His voice tailed off. Mel was appalled.

'You won it playing cards?' She turned to the Doctor, who was still engrossed in the map, and had missed all of this. 'It's a waste of time, Doctor. He won it in a card game.'

'An honest transaction,' protested Glitz. 'The man

was *desperate* not to lose that map. So I knew it must be something *very* tasty.'

The Doctor looked up. 'It appears to show the lower levels of Iceworld.'

The waitress turned to look at the map as well. 'Nobody goes down there now. It's too dangerous.'

The Doctor indicated various places marked on the map, reading them out. 'The Ice Garden ... The Singing Trees ...'

'But like the girl says,' reminded Glitz, 'it's too dangerous.'

'Where's your sense of adventure, Glitz?' demanded the Doctor.

'But look at this ... You don't want to go here, Doctor.' Glitz pointed out some more markings on the map. 'The Lake of Oblivion ...'

'Really? Where's that?' The Doctor looked excitedly at where Glitz's finger was pointing.

Glitz looked for something a bit more frightening. 'The Death of Eternal Darkness ... Dragonfire ... I should stop at home if I were you, Doctor.'

As Glitz read out each dangerous location, the waitress's eyes shone brighter and brighter with excitement. 'Cor – this sounds brill!'

The Doctor turned to her with a smile. 'My sentiments precisely.' He looked at the name patch on her uniform, but it had been torn off. 'Do you have a name?'

'Everyone calls me Ace.'

'Pleased to meet you, Ace. I'm the Doctor – and this is my friend Mel.'

'And we're really off looking for dragons?' Ace's eyes were still shining brightly.

'Too risky, if you ask me,' volunteered Glitz, but the Doctor would have none of it.

'Nonsense, Glitz. We've just time for a quick adventure, and then back in time for tea.'

'Ace!' exclaimed Ace, jumping up.

'That's the spirit, Doctor!' joined in Mel, also jumping up eagerly.

'Hang about,' complained Glitz. 'You can't go without me. It's *my* map.' He took possession of his map again. 'And I'd rather not have any *girls* coming with us.' He glared particularly at Ace. She turned on him angrily. '*What?*'

'It's too dangerous for girls,' he explained condescendingly.

Ace turned to the Doctor for help. 'Professor . . . ?'

But Glitz was insistent. 'And since it's *my* map . . .'

Ace turned back to him in fury. 'Right, you male chauvinist bilgebag! *Just – you – wait!*' And she stormed off back to Eisenstein, who gave her a sharp telling-off for chatting with the customers.

The Doctor sighed, and sat down again, disappointed. 'Oh dear – and I was so looking forward to meeting a dragon.'

'It's all right, Doctor,' consoled Mel. 'You go ahead. I'll meet you back here.' The Doctor's eyes lit up again. Mel then turned angrily on Glitz. 'And if Glitz burns his fingers in the dragon's fire – well, it serves him right!' And then Mel also stormed off to the bar where Ace was serving.

Glitz smiled at the Doctor. 'Just the two of us, then, Doctor . . .'

In the Cryogenics Chamber, Belázs watched Kane gliding silently amongst the tubes of frozen mercenaries. He was like a spectre floating amongst an army of the dead. He spoke. 'Only two of them, you say?'

'Glitz and the traveller called the Doctor. They're just setting off for the Lower Levels.'

'Excellent. Continue to monitor the tracking device.'

'Yes, sir.'

Belázs waited, wondering how she could say this.

Kane noticed she was still there, and looked at her. 'Well?'

Belázs was nervous. 'It's Glitz's spacecraft . . .'

Kane sensed Belázs's fear, and advanced out of the shadows towards her. 'What of it?'

'It's . . .' Faced with those penetrating black eyes, Belázs's courage deserted her.

'Yes?'

'Well, if Glitz and the Doctor are as good as dead . . .' She screwed up her courage and took a deep breath: 'I'd like the spacecraft.'

Kane's silence was like ice.

He stepped towards her like a predator stalking its prey. Belázs watched him warily.

'You'd like the spacecraft, would you?'

Slowly and methodically, Kane began to remove one of his gloves. Belázs was filled with terror. She'd seen this happen to other people who'd made an enemy of Kane. They hadn't lived long. Already she could see ice beginning to form on Kane's flesh. There seemed to be a slight smile on his face. His voice had dropped to an icy whisper.

'When you first came here, you had nothing. You were willing enough to join me then – willing enough to take my payment. But now you want to leave.' He was circling behind Belázs, out of her sight. She was frozen with fear. All she could hear was the evil whisper over her shoulder. 'Perhaps you have memories of home. Perhaps you think you can return home. Perhaps I should have put you into cryo-sleep along with all the others, and erased your memories. Perhaps you need reminding . . .'

Suddenly, he grabbed Belázs's arm with his gloved hand, and forced her palm down onto a control panel. Then, slowly, he lowered his ungloved hand down towards hers. She was trying to fight back her terror, but already she could feel the back of her hand beginning to

26

blister from the deadly freezing cold of Kane's flesh hovering barely a centimetre above hers. With a sudden movement, he pressed his hand down. Belázs stiffened in anticipation of the pain.

But Kane hadn't pressed his bare flesh against hers. Instead there was a hiss as his hand made contact with the metal of the control panel instead. With his gloved hand he wrenched her palm upwards. She saw the deep scar of Kane's insignia branded on her own palm.

'*I own you.* Never forget that. For as long as you bear my mark, I *own* you.'

He tossed her arm aside and strode quickly to the intercom, where he jabbed at a button. Kracauer's voice crackled back in response. 'Yes, sir?'

Kane looked at Belázs while he gave Kracauer his order. 'Glitz's spacecraft – have it destroyed.'

CHAPTER FOUR

Stellar was happy now. Her mother had finally finished trudging around the Freezer Centre and had agreed to buy them both a milkshake. Ace served the two drinks, and then returned to the bar where Mel was sitting.

Ace and Mel were both in a foul mood. Their temper wasn't improved by a distant cheery announcement from the *Bing-bong* Woman: 'Would the Emergency Services please report to the Upper Docking Bays and deal with an icefall? Thank you.' *Bing-bong*.

'This is all *your* fault,' complained Mel.

'How do you work that out, then?'

'You were encouraging them both, with your *Oh, ace! Oh, brill!*'

Ace glared at Mel, and toyed with the idea of pulling her hair out, but she was interrupted by Stellar's mother calling from the table.

'You girl!'

Ace looked round, to make sure that the woman was actually calling her.

'Yes, you girl. Come here!'

Rather unwillingly, Ace wandered over to the customer. 'What do you want?' she asked insolently. The woman took Stellar's milkshake and brandished it beneath Ace's nose.

'This milkshake,' she complained. 'It isn't adequately shaken.'

Ace peered into the milkshake. There didn't seem to be anything wrong with it. 'That's how they come, missus.'

'It's got lumps in it!'

'It's supposed to have lumps in it. That's the ice cream.'

'We don't want lumps in it. Shake it some more!'

Ace was fed up with this complaining woman decorated with ridiculous feathers. 'Shake it yourself!'

'I beg your pardon!'

'You heard!'

'I've never been so insulted . . .'

'I bet you've never had a milkshake tipped over your head before, neither . . .' Ace snatched the tumbler from under her nose and tipped it over the woman's head. The woman shrieked as the cold liquid ran down inside her clothes and down her back. The offending lumps of half-melted ice cream, meanwhile, dribbled slowly down her face and onto the outrageous black feathers that decorated her clothing. Stellar squeaked with delight. This was definitely more fun than wandering round a boring freezer centre!

Mr Eisenstein, standing at the bar, watched all this in horror. Coming to his senses, he strode over to Ace. His face was scarlet. 'That does it! You're fired!'

Ace looked at the soggy mess that was making spluttering noises from beneath the drooping feathers, and she realised that she'd gone too far this time. 'I'm sorry, Mr Eisenstein, it won't happen again.'

Eisenstein's face was now beginning to turn a rather vivid purple. 'Get out! I've had enough of you!'

'I promise, it'll never happen again . . .' Ace desperately needed the job.

'Get out!'

There was no point arguing. Ace knew she'd lost her job.

Eisenstein then turned on Ace's friend, Mel, who had

29

been watching all this from the bar. 'You too! Get out!'

'Me?' Mel wasn't sure what she had to do with any of it.

'Both of you, out! Pair of troublemakers!'

Mel decided not to argue, and she scurried after Ace, who was trudging through the door. 'Hooligans!' shouted Eisenstein after them.

The soggy mess was still squawking pathetically from beneath her bedraggled feathers. Eisenstein turned to her. 'I do apologise, Madam. I hope your delightful outfit wasn't brand new...' Stellar giggled.

The *Bing-bong* Woman, of course, hadn't seen any of this, and another cheery announcement drifted through the Refreshment Bar. 'Would customers please avoid the Upper Docking Bays, which are blocked by an icefall? Thank you.' *Bing-bong.*

There was no longer any tapping sound in Kane's Restricted Zone, and the half-completed ice statue stood shrouded in muslin. Kane was alone, gazing on the veiled statue. He ran his hand softly over the muslin. He seemed to be thinking of something. Something far away.

He shook his head quickly, and turned towards the cabinet. He jabbed at a button, and the transparent lid of the cabinet rose. The mist of supercooled gases flowed out.

Kane slid into the cabinet and lay down. The lid closed, and he felt the refreshing cool of the refrigerating gases as they flowed over him. He crossed his arms across his chest and closed his eyes. He lay like a lifeless body in a coffin. An automatic voice intoned as the temperature inside the cabinet fell. 'Current cabinet temperature: minus 20°C... Target temperature: minus 193°C... Cabinet temperature falling... minus 30°C... minus 40°C...' The voice continued...

From the shadows, Belázs watched. Anyone entering

Kane's Restricted Zone would be killed, but she had followed him. She wanted to know what he kept hidden here.

She turned and retraced her steps back towards the Control Room. The way from the Restricted Zone emerged almost unnoticed into a corner of the Control Room where she strode over to the intercom and pressed the call-button. It was Kracauer's voice that replied. 'Yes, sir?'

'Kracauer, it's me – Belázs. Mr Kane has changed his mind about Glitz's spacecraft. It's *not* to be destroyed. Do you understand?'

There was a short pause, as though Kracauer was thinking about this. Then he confirmed the instruction. 'The spacecraft is not to be destroyed.'

'That is correct.' Belázs released the intercom button. Did Kracauer suspect? If Kane ever found out what she had just done . . .

She looked at the palm of her hand, with Kane's mark branded deeply into her flesh.

After the Doctor and Glitz had left the Refreshment Bar, they had made their way down towards the Staff Quarters, where all the employees in Iceworld lived in small rooms off long corridors. From there, the two adventurers had clambered down the service shafts to reach the Ice Passages that ran beneath Iceworld. Here, a superstructure of metal gantries and walkways had been built onto the solid ice walls and floors. Dim lights illuminated the passages, and threw enough light on Glitz's map for the Doctor to read it. 'See any Ice Gardens, or Singing Trees?' he enquired, peering at the faded writing.

'We're still too close to the Upper Levels, Doctor. Let's cast me eyes over the map.' The Doctor passed the map to Glitz, and looked round, trying to match the gloomy passage to the map.

31

'Well, we've just come from that direction...' he observed looking behind them, 'so I would suggest *that* direction.' He pointed into the darkness ahead of them with his brolly.

'After you, then, Doctor.'

The Doctor strode purposefully off. 'Keep your eyes peeled for Singing Trees and Ice Gardens, Glitz...'

Not long afterwards, Mel and Ace also made their way down the long corridors of the Staff Quarters. Having lost her job, Ace was going back to her room to be miserable. Mel didn't have anything else to do, so she was following on behind.

Ace reached an automatic door, just like all the dozens of other automatic doors on that corridor, and she keyed a number into the security control. The door hissed open, and Ace went inside. Mel peered in at the doorway, not certain whether she had been invited in or not.

Ace's room was the usual teenage pigsty. There were clothes everywhere, with odd balls of discarded underwear strewn across the floor and disappearing under the bed. The room was also full of chemistry equipment, set up for elaborate experiments. Various stains on the floor and walls were evidence of experiments gone wrong, and foul liquids sat congealing in flasks and tubes. Even a poster, saying *There's No Place Like Home*, now had chemical equations scrawled all over it. An official picture of Kane had had two fangs added to it in fibre-tip.

Ace flopped onto the bed and sighed. Then she noticed Mel hovering in the doorway. 'Well, come in then, if you're going to.'

Mel stepped inside, and the door closed behind her. She began to pick her way through the mess on the floor towards a chair. Ace was staring at a recent stain on the ceiling. 'He really gets up my nostrils, that Glitz.'

'Oh, he's all right underneath.'

'No, I'll tell you what he is underneath. He's a Grade A, 100 per cent *div*, that's what he is,' retorted Ace. '*It's too dangerous for girls*,' she mimicked.

Mel was trying to tidy some of the clothes on the chair before sitting down. Ace turned to her in irritation. 'Look, leave them alone, will you?'

'I was only trying to make room to sit.'

'Well, just sit on top of them, can't you, like everyone else does.'

'All right, all right.' Mel didn't feel like getting into another argument with Ace.

Ace relented. 'Well ... I've been meaning to do the washing for a few days.'

Mel looked at the heaps of clothing. 'It looks more like a few weeks.'

Ace turned angrily on Mel. 'All right, then – a few weeks! Satisfied?'

'Sorry ...'

'God, you're just like the teachers at school used to be. They were always complaining: *How do you expect to pass Chemistry A-level if you can't even store the equipment properly?*' Ace sank back onto the bed, miserable. Mel turned to her in surprise.

'A-level? That means you must be from Earth!'

'*Used* to be,' corrected Ace.

'Whereabouts on Earth?'

'Perivale.'

'Sounds a nice place.'

Ace turned to look at Mel. 'You ever been there?' She stood up and started rummaging through the heaps of clothes for something to wear instead of her Iceworld waitress's uniform. She continued talking while she was getting changed. 'I was doing this brill experiment in my bedroom to extract nitroglycerin from gelignite, but I think something must have gone wrong because this time storm blows up from out of nowhere and whisks me

33

here.'

'When was this?'

'Does it matter?'

'Don't you want to go back?'

'Not particularly.'

'What about your Mum and Dad? Won't they be worried?'

Ace spun round, blazing furiously, 'I don't *have* no Mum and Dad! I've *never* had no Mum and Dad! And I don't *want* no Mum and Dad! It's just *me*! Got that?'

Mel was startled by the sudden fierceness. Ace had seemed so tough before. Mel hadn't realised the teenager could suddenly get so upset. Then she remembered what she'd been like herself when she was a teenager: all tough and argumentative on the outside, but sometimes confused and upset inside. 'I'm sorry... I didn't realise...' Ace relaxed slightly, and continued pulling her bomber jacket on. Mel decided to change the subject back to something that Ace was more comfortable with. 'What about Chemistry A-level, then? Don't you want to go back for that?'

'That's no good, either,' said Ace bitterly. 'I got suspended after I blew up the Art Room.'

'You blew up the Art Room?'

'It was only a *small* explosion. But they couldn't understand how blowing up the Art Room was a creative act. All they cared about was how the First Years' pottery pigs got blown through the wall and halfway across the sports field. So they suspended me.'

Even down here in the Staff Quarters, it was impossible to get away from the *Bing-bong* Woman, and she chimed up again with another cheery announcement about the icefall in the Upper Docking Bays. 'If there's anyone on the Emergency Control Room, could you *please* answer the phone? Thank you.' *Bing-bong*.

Ace looked up irritably. 'Isn't *anyone* going to do anything about that flaming icefall?'

34

She turned to the dressing-table and started gathering up some battered aerosol canisters, which she put in a plastic Iceworld carrier-bag and handed to Mel. 'Here – take these.' Mel peered inside and read the lettering on one of the cans: *Iceworld Forest Fragrance Deodorant*.

'Deodorant?'

'They're just old cans.' Ace was stuffing ropes, fuel canisters, and other odds and ends into a canvas shoulder bag. 'They've got home-made nitro-9 in them now,' she continued.

'Nitro-9?' asked Mel, peering suspiciously at the cans.

'It's just like ordinary nitroglycerin – except it's got more wallop. Careful you don't drop them.' Ace grabbed the shoulder bag, and disappeared through the door. Mel wasn't sure whether to drop the cans and run like hell, or hang on to them for grim death.

'Come *on*!' called Ace from the corridor.

Gingerly, Mel stepped through the doorway.

Cautiously, Belázs opened the small door in Kane's Control Room and stepped through into the Restricted Zone. She knew her way and moved quickly through the gloom towards the bright area where Kane's cabinet stood. Kane was still lying there. The automatic voice was no longer intoning the temperature within the cabinet. Belázs was certain she knew what the cabinet was for – why no one was allowed in the Restricted Zone. Even here in the chill of Iceworld it was too warm for Kane. He must come from one of the frozen planets, and he couldn't allow his blood temperature to rise too high. This cabinet was his refrigeration unit. But what was the tall object draped in muslin? Belázs wanted to know.

Silently, she stepped forward. The crisp ice crackled slightly beneath her feet, but Kane lay motionless. She took a corner of the muslin and lifted it. Underneath, she saw a huge block of clear ice. Parts of it had been shaped into a figure, and it seemed to have the rough outlines of a woman.

'What are you doing in the Restricted Zone?'

Belázs's heart stopped.

'I said – what are you doing in the Resticted Zone?'

She felt Kane's cold chill standing behind her. 'I . . . I was looking for you.' She turned to face Kane. 'There's been an icefall in the Upper Docking Bays, and the Emergency Services haven't responded . . .' What was the point of lying? Kane would kill her for this.

His eyes burned into her, cutting right to her soul. She suddenly remembered the first time he had ever looked at her, nearly twenty years ago, when she first arrived in Iceworld. She had just run away from home, and was grateful for work. She was a fresh young teenager then. Kane's wishes had been like sharp needles of ice in her conscience, but she had let him use her – until she was no longer young, no longer fresh. Now he was going to kill her.

Kane's eyes burned right to her memories.

'Must I do everything myself, Belázs? Go there immediately, and take charge of the situation.'

'Yes, sir.' Her mind was numb. She couldn't understand.

She turned to leave.

'And, Belázs . . .'

She turned back.

'This is the last time you will ever set foot inside the Restricted Zone.'

She felt the sickness of death churn within her stomach – and she understood.

The Doctor and Glitz had now journeyed even deeper beneath Iceworld. There were no longer any metal walkways to guide them, and they had to slip and clamber down the shadowy black ice of the Ice Passages. Their way was illuminated by a light that escaped through cracks in the ice. It seemed to come from deep down beneath them. The passages echoed all around with a distant thundering rumble. The Doctor and Glitz followed one passage until it reached a dead end.

'Do you suppose this is the Tunnel of Oblivion, then, Doctor?' asked Glitz, looking at the ice in front of them.

'It's a *Lake* of Oblivion,' corrected the Doctor. 'And according to this map, we should be able to get through here.'

Glitz examined the ice ahead of them. 'It looks like there's been some kind of cave-in. We'll never manage to dig through it.'

'What about through here?' The Doctor was trying to squeeze through a huge crack that ran from top to bottom of the wall to one side. 'The cave-in seems to have fractured the ice just here, and we can probably get through to the other side.'

The cracked ice was rough in places, and the wall was a couple of metres thick, but the Doctor managed to squeeze through, emerging on the other side into a huge ice cavern.

Light strings of ice hung down from the roof of the cavern high above him, and they swayed in the currents of air. There seemed to be the faint sound of voices singing, far away in the breeze. Large crystals shaped in regular polygons clustered on the ground, interconnected by veins of metallic minerals that glittered on the surface. The Doctor looked round, listening to the singing voices, while Glitz scrambled through after him. 'I think we've just found the Singing Trees, Glitz,' he murmured.

Glitz looked round as well. 'These aren't trees.'

'Use your imagination, Glitz. Up there...' The Doctor gestured towards the strings of ice that were hanging down. 'Willow trees – something like that...'

'Yeah, I see what a fertile mind might make of it. But where's the singing coming from?'

'Air currents, I imagine. Causes the crystal membranes to vibrate.'

'I bet it's worth a crown or two.' Glitz surreptitiously pocketed a couple of large crystals and a lump of valuable-looking mineral.

'Beautiful, isn't it? But I wonder what it *does*?'

'*Does?*'

'Yes – it's some kind of opto-electronic circuit. But why? What's it doing here?'

'You mean someone built all this?'

'Not humans, certainly. This is beyond human technology.'

'Dragons?'

The Doctor turned to Glitz with a slight twinkle in his eye. 'Possibly.' Glitz shivered. 'Come on, Glitz. I promised Mel we'd be back for tea.' The Doctor strode off towards the other side of the cavern, which closed down into another passage.

Glitz looked round again, thinking of the creatures who had built all this – and he shivered again.

The entrance to the Upper Docking Bays was completely blocked. A roof section had collapsed under the weight of shifting ice and completely crushed the side walls. On the far side, anyone in the Bays was now trapped. The Emergency Services were nowhere to be seen; only a couple of guards appeared, attracted by the commotion. They were trying to lift one of the fallen girders but it was obviously too heavy for them.

Ace came careering down the corridor and swung round the corner, only to see the mangled passageway ahead of her. Her eyes lit up in delight. 'Gordon Bennett! What a heap of acne!' Mel caught up with her, trying not to jolt the canisters of nitro-9. Ace pointed to the two guards. 'Have you ever seen such a couple of spots! It'll take them *months* to shift it all at that rate! Here – let me have those cans.' She exchanged the canvas shoulder-bag she was carrying for Mel's bag of explosives. Mel looked worried.

'You're not going to *use* those, are you?'

Ace grinned, and nodded. Then she fished two cans out of the bag, and marched up to the icefall. She smiled at the two guards, and carefully positioned the canisters. One of the guards turned to her. 'What's going on?'

'If I were you two, I'd go for your tea-break now.'

'Why?' The guard looked suspiciously at the cans of deodorant. 'What's in those cans?'

'Nitro-9.' Ace smiled defiantly at the guard, then she calmly pulled the nozzle off one can, then the second. The guards stared at the wires they could now see sticking out of the top of each canister, leading to the detonators inside. Ace stood up, and smiled again. 'We've got eight seconds. Last one back's a gooey mess!' and she dived for cover round the corner.

The guard couldn't quite believe what was happening. If he had understood the situation correctly, a teenage girl had just positioned two canisters of nitroglycerin-9, then pulled out the detonator safety pins. Yes, that seemed about the size of it . . .

'*It's nitro!* Everybody get down!' he bellowed, before hurling himself round the corner.

The explosion shook the entire Docking Bays area and blew the fallen ice and metalwork clean through the entrance. There were clouds of smoke and dust everywhere. Ace jumped up, and peered round the corner at the debris that was scattered all over the Docking Bays. Her face blazed with delight as she surveyed the results of her handiwork. '*Ace!*'

CHAPTER FIVE

The Ice Passages were now loose and crumbling; the Doctor and Glitz slipped and fell as they picked their way through the ice boulders.

'Oh, this is definitely out of order,' muttered Glitz, and then yelped as he slipped again. 'Look out!' he cried, as his legs disappeared from under him. He grabbed at a small shaft of ice protruding from the wall, and for a moment he was able to steady himself. But the loosely packed ice wall quickly gave way under his weight, and slabs of ice fractured away and fell towards him.

'Glitz!' shouted the Doctor in alarm from further back down the passage.

As the supporting wall crumbled away, the roof of the passage also began to splinter. Glitz was pinned down by a huge slab of ice that had sheered away from the wall. Sharp, cutting spikes of ice rained down on him, and the weight of the slab of ice crushed his chest. Another large ice shaft collapsed out of the roof, and shattered on the slab of ice.

As the ferocity of the cave-in began to die down, the Doctor hurried forward to help his companion. There were small cuts on his face and hands, but mostly Glitz had been protected by the huge slab of ice that was pinning him down. A large, razor-sharp shaft of ice, however, was now hanging precariously over him. If it fell, the rogue would never walk away.

'Glitz – are you all right?'

Glitz eyed the ice spike hanging over him. 'Er – can I come back to you on that one?' He tried to move, but the slab of ice held him trapped. 'I seem to be stuck.'

'Hang on.' The Doctor began to heave at the slab of ice. He managed to raise it a couple of centimetres, but as he moved it, its base pressed against the ice wall, which started to crumble again.

'Look out!' cried Glitz.

The Doctor flinched as the roof began to slip again and then settled down. The spike of ice had dropped another few centimetres towards Glitz. Glitz looked at it, and then at the Doctor. 'On the whole, I think I'd rather be losing at cards ...'

'Don't worry, Glitz – soon have you out of there ... Now, if we can just raise this a few more centimetres ...' The Doctor began straining once more at the slab of ice.

'You're going to do yourself a permanent, if you're not careful,' observed Glitz, none too helpfully.

The Doctor was still straining to lift the huge slab. 'I said ... I'd have you ... out of there ...' The slab slipped slightly, and the walls and roof settled again. The shaft of ice over Glitz dropped a few more centimetres towards him.

Glitz looked nervously at the Doctor. 'What odds you offering?'

Dust-covered figures were picking their way cautiously through the smoke and debris in the Upper Docking Bays. Mel poked her head nervously round the corner to look. She carefully picked up the bag of nitro, and went over to Ace. Ace was beaming brightly as she surveyed the chaos. 'That was well wicked!'

'What's going on?' Belázs's commanding voice rang through the Docking Bays. She had heard the sound of the explosion from several corridors away and had run here to find a scene of complete devastation. 'Who used explosives?' she demanded, turning to the guards. The guards turned to look accusingly at Ace. Ace tried her best to look innocent, but the effect was spoiled rather by Mel clutching nervously at several cans of high explosive.

'You two are under arrest!' Belázs then turned to the guards. 'Take them away!'

The guards grabbed hold of Ace and Mel.

'Hang about!' protested Ace. 'What have we done?' But the guards hauled them off, Ace squawking in protest. 'You can't arrest us! We haven't done nothing!'

'What we need are some wedges,' muttered the Doctor, looking at the loose rocks in the wall of the Ice Passage.

'I would help you,' offered Glitz from beneath the enormous slab of ice, 'but I'm a bit tied down at this precise moment...'

The Doctor began to pick up wedge-shaped pieces of ice from the ground and pack them into the gaps in the ice wall. 'This should help stop the wall from crumbling while we get you free.' Next he turned his attention to the slab of ice that held Glitz trapped. 'Lever,' he muttered, 'that's what we need – first order lever...' He looked round. 'Fulcrum... we need a fulcrum, Glitz.'

Glitz looked round as well. He didn't like to ask what a fulcrum was, but he was pretty certain there weren't any lying about down here in the Ice Passages. 'Ah, there we are,' announced the Doctor, marching over to what looked like an ordinary rock of ice.

He took the rock and put it down near one end of the slab of ice. Then he wedged the point of his brolly under the slab, and began to lever it against the rock of ice. The slab lifted slightly.

The loose rocks in the wall, which the Doctor had wedged in place, began to shift under the strain. He leaned on the handle of his brolly once more. The shaft of the brolly started to bend under the weight, and two of

42

the Doctor's wedges in the wall shattered, as the rocks shifted ominously. Glitz looked at the point hanging right over him.

'Come on, Doctor – extract your digit, before I get perforated!'

There was now a centimetre and a half of free space between the enormous slab and Glitz. He tried to wriggle free, but it wasn't quite enough room. The Doctor applied all of his weight to the brolly. The slab moved another couple of centimetres. The remaining wedges in the wall shattered, and the roof began to splinter. Glitz wriggled frantically, and slowly started to work himself free of the slab. Rocks of ice began to fall.

Glitz had worked his chest out from under the slab. His legs were now free, and the Doctor continued to heave down on the lever while Glitz scrambled out. The ice shaft fractured at the top, and came crashing down. Glitz and the Doctor both threw themselves out of the way as the huge spike shattered into the ground, precisely where Glitz had been lying.

'Come on, Doctor! Let's get out of here!'

'Just a moment!' The Doctor grabbed his brolly from under the splinters of ice. 'Never know when it might come in useful again...' Then the two of them scrambled away from the danger area.

They stopped to recover further down the passage. Glitz inspected his cuts. There was no serious injury.

'I don't understand you, Doctor. If you'd left me, you could have had the treasure all to yourself.'

'Fortunately, Glitz, not everybody thinks along those lines.'

Glitz looked at the short man with a peculiar face, wearing a battered hat and carrying a brolly, who'd just saved his life. 'You're an odd fish, aren't you, Doctor?'

The Doctor took this for a compliment, and shuffled a bit awkwardly. 'Well – thank you... It brings out the best in me, you know... when I know someone's relying on me...'

'Relying on you? Nah, you're mistaken. I never rely on anyone. Come on, let's get after those Ice Gardens...' And with that, Glitz strode off over the ice boulders.

'Quite a little expert with explosives, I hear...'

Kane prowled round Ace and Mel with a sinister smile. They had been brought to him in the Cryogenics Chamber so that he could meet the troublemakers from the Upper Docking Bays.

'Yeah? So what if I am?' Ace stared defiantly back at Kane.

'Excellent. I like women with fire in their bellies. Don't I, Belázs?' Belázs standing guard over Mel and Ace, refused to acknowledge Kane's question. Her eyes spat jealousy at the fresh, young teenager who had caught Kane's eye. Kane turned back to Ace. 'I might have a use for you...'

'Oh yeah? And what makes you think I'd be interested in you.' Ace had decided this man with the piercing black eyes was taking too much for granted.

'I can be very persuasive...'

'I'm not frightened of you,' lied Ace.

'Good. Because I need people like you in my army of mercenaries.'

'You what?'

'Think about it...' Kane fixed her with his mesmerising gaze. 'Travelling round the Twelve Galaxies... the diamond sparkle of a meteorite shower... the rainbow flashes of an ion storm... think about it...' Ace *was* thinking about it – thinking about all the beautiful things in the universe which she had never seen.

'Don't listen to him, Ace,' pleaded Mel.

Kane nodded to Belázs, who pulled Mel roughly out of the way. Kane turned back to Ace. The teenager was torn between Mel and Kane. She knew Mel was probably right, and yet ... She desperately wanted to see something beautiful in her life. Just once ... Just once, let the little girl from Perivale see something truly beautiful. Kane's eyes read her thoughts. 'How old are you?'

She looked at him, frightened. 'Sixt– No – *eight*een.' She wasn't going to let him think that she was just a small girl. Kane smiled.

'Eighteen, eh? And no home to call your own?' His voice dropped to an intense, intimate whisper. 'The Twelve Galaxies are your home! Come with me. I *understand* you.'

'It won't be like that, Ace!' shouted Mel from the other side of the chamber. 'Don't believe him!'

But Ace didn't hear her. All she heard were Kane's soft, intoxicating words.

'Come with me. Let me show you things that you have only seen in the shadows of your dreams. Let me open you to experiences so beautiful that your tears will flow like liquid crystals. Let me take you home ...' Slowly, Kane removed a glove. Inside, he was holding a golden sovereign. 'Join me. Take my golden sovereign ...'

Ace was transfixed. She watched as Kane placed the sovereign on the Control Desk. There was a slight hiss as it made contact. Slowly, she reached towards it.

She was crying silently.

As the Doctor and Glitz journeyed deeper and deeper beneath Iceworld, they realised that the dim light was growing brighter. Instead of dark shadowy ice, the passages now seemed to be suffused with a soft rainbow glow – a shifting play of gentle colours that filtered through the walls and roof of ice, and sparkled in the light sprinkle of snow on the ground. Side passages led away every few metres, and echoed with the bright crystalline chinkle of icicles.

Glitz helped the Doctor down over an outcrop of ice.

'Mind how you go, Doctor.'

'I should have brought my furry snow boots,' joked the Doctor.

But Glitz had noticed something shimmering in a small crack in the ice. He bent down to examine it. It was a small cluster of crystals, grouped together like a tiny flower. *The Ice Gardens!* thought Glitz. He looked round and saw another tiny flower sparkling on the wall of a side passage, and further down the passage he could see more of them. He looked for the Doctor, who was striding away without having noticed a thing. Glitz quickly nipped down the side passage, dusting over his footprints in the snow to leave no trail, and in a moment he was gone.

'Don't forget to keep your eyes peeled, Glitz!' called the Doctor. 'I should hate to walk right past a Lake of Oblivion and not notice it.' There was no reply. The Doctor stopped and looked round. He was alone. 'Glitz?' There was no reply.

'Glitz!' Still no response. The Doctor made his way back to the outcrop of ice. There were three side passages leading in different directions, and no sign of which way Glitz had gone. The Doctor chose one at random, and set off down it.

It was the wrong one.

Ace's hand hovered over the golden sovereign.

Belázs felt the deep scar in the palm of her own hand. *Don't touch the coin! Run away, child – now! Run from Kane, and never come back!*

'Take the coin,' whispered Kane urgently.

Ace's hand shook uncertainly. The tears left their tracks on her cheeks. Why *shouldn't* she take the coin? Why *shouldn't* she give herself to Kane. Even if he *was* evil – at least he wanted her. No one else had ever cared about her.

'Take the coin.' Kane's voice was more insistent now.

He was growing impatient with the girl. 'Take the coin. Do as you are told.'

Do as you are told!

That was what they all said to Ace – *Do as you are told and learn your lessons, like a good pupil*, the teachers had said. *Do as you are told and go to your bedroom, like a good daughter*, her parents had said. *Do as you are told and give yourself to me, like a good girl*, Kane's voice now said.

Do as you are told! the voices screamed.

DO AS YOU ARE TOLD!

Ace reached suddenly foward, and dashed the coin to the ground. She grabbed a canister of nitro from out of her jacket pocket, and held it high. The hot tears were streaming down her face.

'Nobody move!' she yelled. 'Let Mel go!'

Kane nodded to Belázs, and Mel ran across to Ace.

'You stupid girl.' Kane's voice hissed with hate. 'Do you think it's that easy to walk away from me?'

'If I take the cap off this can, nothing in the universe will matter any more! Come on, Mel.' Mel and Ace edged slowly back towards the door. Kane watched them as the door closed in front of them.

Once out in the corridor, Ace turned quickly to Mel. 'For God's sake, run!'

Glitz followed the trail of tiny, flower-like crystals as it led through the passages and finally opened out into a huge cavern with a roof that curved overhead in an immense dome. The darkness of the cavern was patterned with the bright glitter of the tiny crystal flowers. Hundreds of tiny sparkles spread out above Glitz like stars in the night sky. The Ice Garden.

Glitz stared at the patterns above him. There was something familiar about them. He'd seen them before somewhere.

Of course! The stars in the sky! Now he looked at them, he could make out one or two familiar constellations – the Great Lever, the Old Man, and the Waterfall. They were in unusual positions, and it had evidently all been drawn from a point far beyond the limits of the Twelve Galaxies, but the Ice Gardens were obviously some kind of huge planetarium.

Very pretty – but not exactly the fabulous treasure that Glitz had been hoping for. His business instincts briefly considered the possibility of turning it into a tourist attraction, and organising guided tours for visitors to Iceworld. But he decided that there probably wasn't much money to be made out of that, and in any case Mr Kane would take a dim view of the enterprise if he ever found out. So Glitz turned back the way he had come, to find the Doctor again.

It never occurred to Glitz to wonder *why* there should be a huge planetarium buried deep beneath Iceworld . . .

CHAPTER SIX

The Doctor peered over the edge of the Ice Face. It was a sheer drop of about fifteen metres. The ice glowed with a soft, rainbow iridescence – but the Doctor saw the sharp, jagged ice that would cut him to ribbons before he ever hit the bottom, should he fall. He looked back the way he had come. But which way *had* he come? It had all seemed straightforward as he was progressing forwards, but looking back now, he saw several passages leading in different directions. In any case, these passages all led back up towards the Upper Levels. The only way forwards was down.

He peered over the edge again. There seemed to be large enough cracks in the ice to use as hand- and foot-holds. But they were too widely spaced. He would have to use his brolly again, hooking into the handholds to steady him until he reached the next one.

He found a secure ledge at the top, and hooked the handle of the brolly over it. Then he turned round, and carefully began to feel his way down the Ice Face with his first foot until he found a secure footing. He held onto the ledge and felt down with his second foot until that too was secure in a foothold.

Gripping onto his brolly now, he carefully removed his first foot from its hold and felt further down for another hold. At the same time, he released one hand to feel round for a lower handhold. He secured his foot, and then steadied himself with the new handhold.

Looking up, he unhooked the brolly, and carefully lowered it until the handle was planted firmly in the lower hand-hold. He now removed his second foot, and felt downwards for a new crack. As he was doing this, he felt the ice beneath his first foot beginning to crumble. He clung tightly onto his brolly. The ice gave way beneath his secure foot, and he fell free. The only thing to prevent him from falling to his death was his brolly, and he was left hanging from it.

He tried to look down, but his arms got in the way. He felt round with his feet for a secure crack that would take his weight, but he found nothing.

He was left swinging helplessly.

Kane turned to Belázs in anger. 'You astound me! You didn't even think to search the two girls when you arrested them!'

'I wasn't expecting her to be carrying nitro.'

'She'd just blown away half of the Upper Docking Bays! Of course she was likely to be carrying explosives! And you carelessly allowed her to bring them close enough to my person to kill me!' Kane began to close in on Belázs. 'You seem to be taking advantage of my former feelings for you. Be warned... the past is an empty slate. I demand absolute loyalty – now and forever. And I do not forgive those who betray me.' He turned to the Control Desk, and jabbed at a button. The five tubes containing the frozen figures of Glitz's former crew began to glow inside. 'The two girls must be stopped – *before* they reach Glitz and the Doctor. They must be... eradicated.' He pressed another sequence of controls, and the five tubes began to rise. 'What could be more appropriate than to despatch Glitz's former crew after them? He betrayed his crew – now they can have their revenge! Every man must be allowed his moment of revenge...'

The five figures lurched forward from beneath the tubes. Their faces were dead and empty, save for the dull, murderous gaze in their eyes. Together, they staggered through the door, after Mel and Ace. Kane watched them go. He had hundreds of psychopathic zombies like these at his command ...

Ace knew that she and Mel weren't safe in Iceworld with guards everywhere, so she'd made straight for the Ice Passages beneath the colony. This was where the Doctor and Glitz had come looking for the fairy tale dragon. This was where all the excitement would be. 'Hurry up!' she shouted back to Mel. 'Or we'll miss everything!'

They had now left the safety of the passages directly beneath the Upper Levels, with their metal walkways and ladders, and were making their way through the treacherous black ice. Mel looked round nervously. 'Hang on, Ace. Are you sure this is the right way?'

'Course I'm sure.'

'It all looks the same in the dark. We could get lost.'

Ace turned to look at Mel accusingly. 'What's the matter? Don't you trust me?'

'It's not that. It's just that ... Well ... the dragon and all that ...'

Ace laughed. 'The dragon? That's just to frighten little children!' Something moved in the shadows behind Ace. 'It's like witches and goblins. There ain't no such thing!'

A huge creature rose out of the shadows and advanced on Ace. Mel screamed in terror. Ace turned to see the Creature towering over her – tall and skeletal, with greyish-white membranes instead of skin. Two narrow red beams of light radiated from its sparkling eyes and burst in a small crackle of fire as they hit the ice. It didn't look anything like a dragon, but this was it!

Ace's eyes lit up with excitement. 'Mega!'

The Creature turned towards Ace and the two beams of fire burst at her feet.

'Get down!' yelled Mel.

The two women dived for cover behind some ice boulders. As the Creature stepped forward, they could see it more clearly. It had a large bony skull on top of a long neck and its skeleton was clearly visible beneath the membranous skin. It turned to the boulders where Mel and Ace were hiding and its twin beams of fire crackled once again as they burst into the ice.

'That's not a dragon,' complained Ace. 'And it's not breathing real fire! It's just some kind of bio-mechanoid, with laser beams or something coming out its eyes!' She stood up and glared at the Creature angrily. Genuine dragon or not, the Creature rounded on Ace. Mel dragged her down behind the ice just as two more beams of fire burst.

Mel turned to Ace. 'What we need now is an ingenious plan to save ourselves.'

'Give me the nitro! It won't know what hit it!'

'Neither will *we*! They'll be shovelling *us* into black plastic bags along with the Creature.'

'Yeah – you're right. There's not enough space. Well... how about... we run like hell!'

'That's ingenious enough!'

So, they ran like hell ... with the Creature's beams of fire bursting all around them.

The Doctor was finding it difficult to hang onto his brolly. His hands ached, but he gritted his teeth and clenched his fingers round the brolly's shaft. He heard a crunching sound from above and a light sprinkling of snow fluttered down onto his head.

Glitz looked down over the edge of the Ice Face. For some reason, the Doctor was hanging from his umbrella. It looked dangerous, but Glitz knew better than to ask questions. He decided to tell the Doctor his good news instead. 'I've located the Ice Garden, Doctor,' he called down. 'But I'm afraid there was a distinct absence of both dragon and treasure.'

The Doctor's hands slipped a couple of centimetres down the brolly. 'I sympathise with your disappointment, Glitz – really I do. But I'm about to plummet to my death!'

Glitz peered down at the Doctor. 'I suppose you'll be wanting me to risk *my* neck and come and help you, then . . .'

'Glitz!' shouted the Doctor crossly.

Glitz jumped, and started to scramble down towards the Doctor. 'All right, all right. Don't get your delicates in a twist!'

The Sculptor was at work again. The ice statue was almost complete. It was a woman with a face that would have looked young were it not for the hard beauty of the eyes. The eyes! The rest of the statue was still and motionless, but the eyes seemed to be alive!

Kane watched the Sculptor at his work. 'A work of artistry, my friend – incandescent artistry. I could almost believe that Xana lives again. The expression in her face – yes . . . The exquisite beauty – yes . . . But more than that . . . The criminal genius also – I see it in her eyes!'

Kane reached forward to touch the statue. He caressed it gently, as if he were touching the real woman's flesh. 'What a waste . . . It should have been *I* who was killed escaping – not you . . .'

The five crewmen and women, sent by Kane to kill Mel and Ace, made swift progress through the Ice Passages. After cryogenesis, they could feel no pain or fear, so where Mel and Ace had slowed down to make their way through the dark passages, the empty-faced murderers lost no time.

Their brains were dead, but – just as every abomination that has returned from the dead is drawn irresistibly towards living creatures, in order to kill them

53

– they somehow knew exactly which turning to take, and which passage to follow.

And with every heavy footfall, they drew steadily closer to their victims.

Mel and Ace had outdistanced the Creature, but were now totally lost in the maze of black ice. Mel kept looking round nervously. 'Do you get the feeling something's watching us?'

'It's just tricks of the light. Shadows dancing in the corner of your eye.'

'Yeah.'

But neither of them was convinced...

Then suddenly, down a side passage, Ace saw a figure move. She spun round towards the figure and pulled a can of nitro out. She was just about to pull the safety nozzle off and throw the can, when Mel grabbed her arm. 'Stop!'

Ace tried to pull her arm free. 'Let go!'

'Don't throw it!' Mel grabbed Ace's arm again. 'Look! See who you're throwing it at...'

Ace stared at the figure down the side passage. She saw herself staring back...

'It's your reflection, Ace!'

Ace looked carefully down the side passage. At the far end stood a wall of absolutely smooth ice, reflecting an image of two women who stared back at Mel and Ace. Ace looked around. There were more reflections in the smooth, black ice sheets. They were like spirits – phantoms mocking the movements of two dead women.

Ace shivered. 'This place is too crafty for my liking. Much too crafty...'

The Doctor and Glitz dropped the last couple of metres down the Ice Face. The Doctor had had to leave his brolly halfway down, when it got jammed, but he picked himself up with a smile of achievement. 'Teamwork –

that's what it takes!' he said, by way of congratulation, and then looked around for a likely route forward.

'It's no use, Doctor.'

The Doctor looked back, and saw Glitz sitting despondently on a boulder at the foot of the Ice Face. 'What's no use?'

'The treasure. Even if we do manage to find it, it's going to take us more than seventy-two hours. And Belázs said that if I don't return Kane's money within seventy-two hours, they'll confiscate my spacecraft.' Glitz didn't realise that, thanks to the radio transmitter hidden in his treasure map, Belázs was listening to everything he now said.

'Perhaps if you were to explain the problem to Kane . . .' offered the Doctor.

'I take it you've never actually made the gentleman's acquaintance?'

The Doctor shook his head.

'He'd slice his mother up to make a point, Doctor. If he was a mortician, the corpses would keep their eyes open.'

'Ah.'

'In fact, if he knew we was after the Dragon's Treasure, your life expectancy wouldn't be looking too clever at the moment. He's a cold man, Doctor. Cut him open, and you won't find a heart – just a lump of ice . . .'

Belázs, listening to the radio tracking equipment, looked up for a moment and thought of twenty years earlier.

The Doctor sat down next to Glitz. 'These types never seem to have any sense of fair play.'

'Exactly, Doctor. And that's why I have come to the conclusion that playing by the rules is a mug's game. I've decided to hijack the *Nosferatu* – which is where *you* come in, Doctor.'

'Now just a moment, Glitz,' protested the Doctor in alarm. 'I'm engaged in a project of scientific curiosity.

The dragon, or whatever it turns out to be, may be an undiscovered species.'

'Look – I'll do you a good deal. If you'll help me get my spacecraft, the *Nosferatu*, back, I'll give you the treasure map so that you and Mel can go looking for this dragon. Now I can't say no fairer than that, can I?'

'Ah.' The Doctor looked crossly at Glitz. 'Without the map, I can't find the creature, can I? I don't seem to have any choice.'

'You're a man of rare insight and logic, Doctor.'

'All right, then. Where's the *Nosferatu* berthed?'

'It's in the Lower Docking Bays – Pier 63.'

Belázs switched the tracking equipment off, and smiled. That was all she needed to know...

The Sculptor lay down his tools, then brushed away the final chippings of ice with his thumb. He turned to Kane.

Kane was transfixed by the fierce beauty of the statue. 'It is finished,' he whispered. He stepped forward and reached towards the face of the statue. 'The whole of eternity has held its breath for this moment. Time has stood motionless. The past is finally obliterated!' He turned to the Sculptor, his voice soft and tender. 'But no one must ever see your work. It *exists* – that is enough. No one can ever be allowed to look on it and live.' Kane started to remove one of his gloves.

The Sculptor watched him. He knew how close he was to death, but he was peaceful. He had always known that he would die like this.

'What more could you achieve with your life?' whispered Kane. 'After this – nothing. You have found your true destiny in life, and fulfilled it. What would be the point of trying to live beyond it?' With his gloved hand, he drew the Sculptor towards him. 'Feel no fear. You are beyond that also. Your death shall be speedy, I promise you. Embrace death with the same tranquil artistry with which you embraced your destiny.' Kane turned the Sculptor away, towards the statue. 'Your final sight shall be that of your ultimate achievement. Gaze on it – and die fulfilled ...'

Solemnly, Kane placed his bare hand over the Sculptor's eyes, and pressed against his face. The Sculptor was instantly blinded by the freezing pain. He had planned for this moment, planned on holding himself utterly calm as his life froze away and turned to ice, but now he was terrified. He tried not to struggle, but the warm-blooded animal instinct in him wanted to fight – fight and preserve every last drop of precious life.

Shortly, the Sculptor's struggles grew weaker, then ended – the body lay limp, cradled in Kane's arms. Kane lowered the body gently to the ground.

He stood back, and gazed up at the statue.

There weren't many passengers in the Lower Docking Bays, and the Doctor and Glitz made their way to Pier 63. The status board indicated that the *Nosferatu* was still berthed there. From behind a cargo pallet, standing at the adjoining pier, they saw a guard waiting by the airlock.

'Only one guard,' whispered Glitz. 'Do you think you can keep him occupied, while I sneak on board?'

The Doctor looked doubtfully at the huge, Neanderthal thug. 'I'll do my best.'

'Right then – off you go.'

The Doctor straightened himself, emerged from behind the cargo pallet, and loped confidently off towards the guard. He strode in a complete circle, and ended up heading back towards the pallet. Glitz watched the manoeuvre in amazement.

The Doctor returned to Glitz's hiding place. 'What's the matter?' hissed Glitz.

'Haven't you forgotten something?'

'What's that?'

'The map.'

Glitz squirmed guiltily. 'I was going to leave it here – for you to find when you got back. Honest I was ...'

The Doctor held his hand out for the map. Reluctantly, Glitz fished it out of his belt, and handed it over. The Doctor put it safely in his pocket. 'Thank you. Right, good luck.' The Doctor held his hand out to shake Glitz's and then set off again towards the guard.

The guard didn't seem to notice the Doctor approaching, and the Doctor glided right past him to stand on his other side. The Doctor decided that the guard was evidently ignoring him, so he cleared his throat. 'Excuse me ...' he started, 'what's your attitude towards the nature of Existence?' Glitz, listening from behind the pallet, raised his eyes in disbelief.

The guard turned and stared at the Doctor.

The Doctor regarded the simian-featured guard and began to doubt whether in fact the guard was high enough up the evolutionary ladder to comprehend spoken language. But he decided to persevere. 'For example: do you hold any strong theological opinions?'

The guard stared at him, then opened his mouth to speak. 'I think most educated people regard mythical convictions as fundamentally animistic,' he grunted.

The Doctor's jaw dropped.

Glitz was incredulous.

The Doctor recovered himself. 'I see ... That's a very interesting concept ...'

The guard spoke again. 'Personally, I find that most experiences border on the existential.'

'Ah. But how would you reconcile that with the empirio-critical belief that experience is at the root of all phenomena?'

Glitz emerged from behind the pallet, and gingerly made his way round the back of the guard towards the open door to the air-lock.

The guard was absorbed by trying to answer the

Doctor's logical conundrum. 'I think you'll find that a concept can be philosophically valid, even if theologically meaningless,' he countered.

This response had the Doctor struggling. 'So, what you're saying is that before Plato could exist, someone had to have the Idea of Plato?'

The guard's face lit up. 'You've no idea what a relief it is for me to have such a stimulating philosophical discussion. There are so few intellectuals about these days.' The Doctor smiled and noticed that Glitz had now disappeared through the door. But the guard had no intention of letting the Doctor leave so soon. 'Tell me – what are *your* views on the assertion that the semiotic thickness of a performed text varies according to the redundancy of auxiliary performance codes?'

Semiotics? The Doctor began to worry. This was going to be a very difficult conversation ...

Ace peered down the sheer drop of the Ice Face.

'You're joking! I'm not going down there!'

Mel saw something hanging halfway down. 'Look – it's the Doctor's brolly! We must be on the right track!'

Ace looked down again. 'What did he have to come this way for? I could break my neck!'

'How are we going to get down?'

Ace put her canvas shoulder bag down, and began to rummage through it. 'Easy!' She produced two coils of rope and various rock-climbing clips and pulleys. 'First, you lower me down. Then, I lower you down from the bottom. Here – sort this out!' She thrust some tangled rope at Mel, then dived into the canvas bag again. While Mel set to, untangling the rope, Alice clipped a harness round herself and looked for a secure place to nail the pulleys into the ground.

'I've never done this before,' admitted Mel. 'You must have done it lots of times.'

'Well, not *lots* of times ...'

Ace was avoiding Mel's eyes.

'How *many* times?' asked Mel suspiciously.

'This'll be the first.' Ace looked up guiltily. 'But I've seen them do it on telly, and it's easy!'

Mel looked at Ace. The safety harness Ace was wearing didn't look quite right. 'I think you've got that harness on upside-down. I think those tight straps are supposed to go between your legs.'

Ace looked down, and giggled. 'It's a good job I'm not a boy!' she laughed. Mel smiled – and then she began to laugh as well. This wasn't going to be a bit like they always showed it on telly!

Ace fixed the harness and clipped one end of the rope to it. She threaded the rope through the pulleys and clips, then gave the other end to Mel. 'Here – stand on the loose rope with one foot, just in case your hands slip.'

'OK.' Mel took hold of the rope, and pressed her heel firmly down on the loose section. Ace stepped backwards towards the edge.

'Right. You got it?'

'Yes, I'm ready.'

Ace leaned backwards, and Mel took her weight.

'Just a bit at a time, Mel – right?'

'I'll let the rope out slowly.'

Carefully, Ace held onto the edge and began to feel downwards with her feet for some kind of foothold. Metre by metre, she started to make her way down the Ice Face, with Mel taking her weight. The operation was both difficult and strenuous, and their faces were tense with concentration. 'You OK?' called Mel in a strained voice.

'Keep going... Slowly... I'm about a third of the way.'

The longer it took, the greater the strain became and Mel's hands started to ache from gripping the rope so tightly. She pressed her heel down even more firmly on the loose rope.

Ace was beginning to lose her breath with the effort of trying to find hand- and foothold while still avoiding the sharp, jagged edges of ice. Suddenly, one of her foothold crumbled and she slipped and banged against the side. At the top, Mel felt the sudden extra weight which pulled her forward. She was alarmed. 'What happened? Ace – are you all right?'

Ace was struggling to recover her foothold and handhold. 'Yeah – I'm OK. Keep going.' Mel steadied herself and gripped tight on the rope. What Ace hadn't noticed was that when she collided with the Ice Face a small spike of ice had punctured one of the two canisters of nitro-9 that were tucked securely in her belt. A light haze of fumes was now escaping from a small hole near the top of the canister. The first that Ace noticed was a sweet, sickly smell she recognised from somewhere. She began to feel giddy and clutched aimlessly at the Ice Face for some security. 'Hang on a sec ...' she called weakly.

Mel heard Ace and held the rope still. 'What's the matter?'

'I feel funny ... I think I'm going to faint ...'

'No! Don't do that! Hang on!' Mel started to tie off the loose end of the rope.

Ace looked down at the canister of nitro-9 and saw the small hole in it. 'It's the nitro, there's a hole in it. I'm going to pass out ...'

'No, don't, Ace! Keep concentrating. I'm coming down!' Mel fastened Ace's rope tightly, then clipped the second harness on to herself.

'Hurry up! I can't think.'

Mel quickly threaded her own rope through the pulley instead of Ace's and took the free end. 'Concentrate on something, Ace! Don't go to sleep!' She grabbed a spare clip and a few first-aid sticking plasters from Ace's canvas bag, then stepped back towards the edge, taking her own weight on the free end of the rope.

Ace was fighting the drowsiness, talking to herself to

stay awake. 'Come on, Ace... Not now... Can't go to sleep now... Hang on, Ace...'

With immense effort, Mel slowly managed to lower herself down the ice face. Her feet kept slipping and there were already one or two small cuts on her hands from scraping against the sharp ice, but she knew that there was no time to spare. 'Keep talking, Ace! I'm on my way down. Just another minute.'

Ace's head dropped briefly as she fell asleep for a moment, but she shook herself awake. 'Come on... Mel's almost here... Keep tight hold...'

With grim determination, Mel was scrambling down towards Ace. 'I'm almost there... Just keep talking!'

Ace's mind was swimming and her thoughts slipped in and out of dreams. How nice it would be to drift away – how pleasant it would be to give in to the hypnotic currents that spiralled through her mind.

'Keep talking to me!' shouted Mel, suddenly alarmed that Ace had stopped talking.

Ace shook herself awake again. 'No! Mustn't fall asleep!' But the dreamy spirals caressed her thoughts again. 'Want to go home...' she murmured, '... bed... home... Mum... Dad...' She shook the strange patterns out of her mind once more. 'No! Too late! Too late, Ace!'

Mel had almost reached Ace and could smell the faint sweetness of the nitro fumes. She turned her face away and took a huge lungful of clean, icy air. It burnt her lungs. She turned back to Ace and lowered herself alongside. The effort was tremendous as she held her own weight with only one arm and reached across to the leaking canister with the other. She pulled it out of Ace's belt and then reached down to hold the canister between her knees. Her lungs were bursting for fresh air, but Mel knew that she mustn't inhale. She fished a sticking plaster out of her pocket and held it between her teeth. The fumes from the canister tasted sweet on her tongue.

She ripped the backing off the plaster, and stuck the adhesive down over the hole in the can. Her lungs were tearing apart for air, but she refused to inhale. She took another plaster and stuck that too over the hole. The leak of fumes had almost stopped. One more plaster should be enough. The muscles in the hand gripping the rope were cramped with pain and her lungs were fighting to wrench themselves free, but somehow Mel forced herself to control the uncontrollable muscles while she stuck a third plaster over the hole and sealed it. Her lungs seemed to explode as she inhaled. She quickly gripped tight on the rope with her free hand to take the strain off the painful hand, carefully holding the canister of nitro secure between her knees.

The cold fresh air, mixed with the last traces of fumes, rushed to her brain. She felt her mind starting to spin slightly, but she concentrated on holding still until her brain began to clear once more.

She looked across to Ace, who seemed to be waking from a groggy sleep and couldn't quite orient herself. Mel took the canister of explosive from between her knees, and tucked it securely into her own belt. Ace had a second canister in her belt, so Mel took that too and secured it in her own. 'Are you ready to go down yet, Ace?'

Ace still felt a bit dizzy, but she knew where she was now, and her mind was clearing rapidly. 'Yeah, I'll be OK.'

'We've got to go down together, on the same rope. Your rope's tied off at the top. Here . . .' Mel passed the spare clip to Ace, who leaned across and fastened herself to Mel's rope.

'Have you got the weight?'

Mel now had to take the strain of both of them on the free end of rope. She gripped both hands tightly, and nodded. Ace unclipped herself from her own rope, and then grabbed hold of Mel's. They were both now clipped

63

together on one end of the rope, both taking the weight on the free end.

With perfect co-ordination, they slowly lowered themselves down towards the bottom. Halfway down they stopped, while Mel reached across and rescued the Doctor's brolly, then continued down to the bottom.

They stood there, breathless but smiling.

'That was well worth...' gasped Ace brightly. 'And Bilgebag said this was too dangerous for girls!'

When the Nightcruiser range of space vehicles had first been launched, over thirty years ago, it had quickly caught on as the most popular vehicle for passenger transport. Every third craft to soar down the Space Lanes had been a Nightcruiser, most of them Nightcruiser Democrats out on family outings, but also quite a few Nightcruiser Pacifics, whisking busy executives between meetings. That was thirty years ago. But then people's tastes had changed; new styles of vehicle were launched, the Nightcruiser's market-share had started to fall, and the last production line had finally been closed down fifteen years ago. Most of these old vehicles now floated in junk orbits round small, barren planets. But a few still survived, either conscientiously maintained by careful owners, or bought cheaply by teenagers who couldn't afford the flashy new models.

The *Nosferatu* was an old Nightcruiser Pacific. Glitz had picked two of them up cheaply twelve years ago, and used spares from one engine to overhaul the other. The cannibalised craft was then involved in a 'tragic' fire, which netted slightly more for Glitz in insurance compensation than he had originally paid for both craft together. Since then, Glitz and the *Nosferatu* had never been apart. His crewmen came and went – mostly went – but the *Nosferatu* stayed loyally with Glitz. It was not only his transport for getting from place to place, it had also become his home, with his cabin transformed into a kind of small bachelor pad used for entertaining.

The *Nosferatu* interior glowed dimly on auxiliary power, as Glitz hurried towards the Flight Cabin. The Doctor would only be able to keep the guard occupied in conversation for a couple of minutes more, and Glitz didn't want to risk being found by the guard if he decided to search the craft.

'Soon be light years away from this place,' he chuckled to himself as he slipped into his seat, and clipped the security belt on.

'I wouldn't touch those controls, if I were you.'

Glitz felt the cold muzzle of Belázs's hand-gun press against his temple. Glitz froze, and tried to squint sideways at Belázs.

'I thought I gave you seventy-two hours to repay the money you owe? I do hope you're not trying to leave without paying your debts.'

'No. Absolutely not. I just ... I just came back here for some necessary equipment. I've got a plan, you see ...'

Belázs started to laugh. 'You and your "plans", Glitz! You're an endless source of amusement – do you know that?'

'Well, I try my best.' Glitz joined in the laughter, hoping that Belázs might take her gun away.

Belázs suddenly stopped laughing. 'But you're not being very amusing now! This spacecraft is *mine*!'

'Here, hang about! The seventy-two hours isn't up yet. You said, if I could get hold of the jumbo, I could have the *Nosferatu* back.'

'In that case, I shall just have to make sure you *don't* manage to find the money in time.' Her finger tightened on the trigger of her gun. 'I shall have to make *very* sure.' She levelled the gun more carefully, and Glitz stiffened.

'Hello! Not interrupting anything, am I?' The Doctor's voice interrupted cheerfully from the hatchway of the Flight Cabin.

Belázs spun round to point the gun at him. 'What are

you doing here?' she demanded.

'A very difficult philosophical question. Why is everyone around here so preoccupied with metaphysics? I've just persuaded your friend outside that experience is causal and existence doubtful. He's probably turned himself into a puff of blue smoke by now. But do carry on ... don't let me interrupt.' The Doctor gaily waved Belázs back to whatever it was she was about to do with the hand-gun when he came in.

'I think she's going to kill us,' said Glitz nervously.

The Doctor looked at the gun again. 'Ah, an existentialist ...'

'Quiet!' commanded Belázs. 'Only one of us can escape from Svartos and Iceworld aboard the *Nosferatu* – and that's going to be *me*!'

'What about the boss – Mr Kane?' asked Glitz. 'Does he know about this little enterprise of yours?'

'Kane and I are finished. All I'm waiting for is the opportunity.'

'Doesn't strike me as the kind of gent who'll let you run off without so much as an *au revoir*.'

Belázs turned angrily on Glitz. 'Kane doesn't *own* me!'

'Oh, I think he does,' disagreed the Doctor, drawing her attention away from Glitz. 'I think he bought you just like he buys everything in Iceworld.'

'What do you know about it?' cried Belázs angrily, as Glitz cautiously began to unfasten his seat belt.

The Doctor saw Glitz, and continued to distract Belázs. 'I think he bought you a long time ago. He paid seventeen crowns each for Glitz's crew. How much did he pay for you?' He saw that Belázs was about to lose her temper, and continued to provoke her. 'How much did you sell yourself for? Was it worth it? Were *you* worth it?'

Belázs was too angry to notice that Glitz had slipped out of his seat belt as she furiously thrust her palm up at the Doctor, brandishing the scar. 'That's what I sold myself for! Kane's mark! I should cut my hand off for doing it!'

Glitz seized his moment and threw himself on Belázs. She saw him come at her and tried to turn her gun on him, but he had the edge and pinned her arm down. He wrenched the gun out of her hand, and once he had it secure in his own grasp, he pushed her away. She fell to the ground. Glitz covered her with the gun.

'Go on, then. Kill me!' she cried, through tears of anger and bitterness.

Glitz turned to the Doctor. 'Come on, Doctor. We've got the *Nosferatu*. Let's get away from here.'

'No, Glitz. You'd be exactly like her then. Forever in Kane's debt. Forever wondering if the movement you think you just saw in the shadows is Kane, come to recover his dues. Pay Kane his money. Even if it costs a thousand crowns. Even ten thousand. Pay off the debt.' The Doctor turned to Belázs. 'Your debt to Kane, I don't think you can *ever* pay off ...'

The Doctor turned and left.

Glitz followed. He felt slightly sorry for the woman they left weeping bitterly on the floor.

The mindless crewmen and women descended the Ice Face without slowing down. Where Mel and Ace had struggled with ropes, and Glitz and the Doctor had inched their way from foothold to foothold, their pursuers climbed down as though the Ice Face were a secure ladder. Wherever they placed their feet, there was a foothold. Wherever they reached their arms, there was a handhold. The razor-sharp ice cut deep into them, but their cold flesh didn't bleed. Like corpses, they staggered onwards. They knew that they were close to the living creatures they must kill.

CHAPTER SEVEN

Ace and Mel were trudging through the gloom of the Ice Passages, but Ace was cheerful. 'My head feels as though I was out on a real bender last night!' she laughed.

'You had a very lucky escape with that nitro,' cautioned Mel.

Ace shrugged. 'You make your own luck in this life.'

Suddenly, she stopped dead in her tracks.

'What's the matter?'

'Shh!'

Mel stopped as well.

'Did you hear that?' whispered Ace.

Mel looked round nervously. 'Hear what?'

Ace peered back into the darkness behind them. 'I'm sure I heard something behind us.'

Mel shivered. 'What kind of something?'

'I don't know. Can you see anything?' Ace turned to look into the darkness ahead of them. As she did so, one of the dead-faced crewmen lurched out of one of the side passages behind them. Mel saw it with horror.

'Look out!' she shrieked.

Ace turned to see the huge abomination. Then another one emerged. Then another one. 'Gordon Bennett!'

Still more crewmen emerged. Mel screamed, but the zombies appeared not to hear. They staggered on down the passage towards Mel and Ace, with murder in their eyes.

Ace looked round wildly. The only escape was forward

down the passage. 'Come on, Mel – run!' She pulled Mel's arm, and they both raced off into the dark. The crewmen and women stumbled after them.

Mel and Ace scrambled over the ice boulders as fast as they could. Behind them, they could hear their pursuers striding over the ice like unstoppable giants. 'They're still behind us! We can't get away!' cried Mel.

Ace felt down to her belt. 'Let's see if they want to argue with a can of deodorant that registers nine on the Richter scale!' But the canisters of nitro were missing. 'The nitro! You've got the nitro, Mel! Throw it!'

The two canisters of nitro were secure in Mel's belt. She pulled them out, and turned back to face the huge crewmen and women. 'Right – cover your ears!' She pulled the nozzle off one of the cans, as she'd seen Ace do in the Upper Docking Bays, then she tossed it down the passage.

It bounced on the ground and came to rest. The crewmen and women strode towards it with dead faces.

The explosion rocked the passage, and the blast of air knocked Mel and Ace to the ground. Ace's eyes lit up with excitement. 'Mega!' she cried in a whoop of delight. 'Go on, Doughnut – throw the other one!'

Mel was really getting the feel of this now. She pulled the nozzle of the second can off with her teeth, like she'd seen them do with hand grenades in old war movies, and with a broad smile she lobbed it after the first. There was a second huge explosion, which knocked the two women backwards. 'Yeah! Go for it, Doughnut!' shrieked Ace, flat on her back. She rolled onto her side and looked down the passage. Amidst a cloud of dust, the crewmen and women were lying buried beneath a mound of ice boulders. Smiling, Ace turned to Mel. 'That was well brill!'

Mel was looking down the passage. 'I don't think we're safe yet.' Ace turned to look.

Back down the passage, the crewmen and women were

beginning to stir beneath the rubble. Ace couldn't believe it. 'They can't be. Not after *two* cans of nitro. Throw the rest, Mel! Throw everything!'

'There's none left! That's all there was.'

'Come on, then – let's shift!'

They scrambled to their feet and ran.

The ice was slippery beneath their feet, and they kept crashing to the ground, picking themselves up again, and hurling themselves forward once more. Always they heard the steady crunch of feet following behind, never dropping any further into the distance. Mel turned briefly to see where their pursuers were. As she did so, her feet flew away from under her, and her head smashed against the side wall. She didn't feel any pain. She just saw everything disappear into black – and then nothing . . .

Ace quickly realised that Mel was no longer running alongside her. She stopped and looked back, and saw Mel lying inert on the ground. 'Doughnut!' She ran back to Mel and dropped down beside her. Blood was running down the side of Mel's head, but she was still breathing. 'Come on! Wake up!' Ace shook Mel. 'Come *on*!' The monotonous crunch of heavy footsteps grew closer in the darkness further up the passage.

Ace looked round in desperation. There were no side passages to hide down – just forwards and backwards. The heavy foosteps crunched closer.

Ace looked frantically up the side walls. About two metres up one of the walls was a deep horizontal crack. Ace didn't know whether it was deep enough to hide in, but there was no alternative. She dragged Mel to the foot of the wall, and tried to haul her to her feet. Mel was petite, but she was still heavy to manhandle. Ace pushed her up the wall, and then kneeled down to get underneath her. She pushed upwards, and slowly Mel's floppy body slid towards the opening. The heavy footsteps grew nearer.

Ace's feet slipped on the ice, as she struggled to push

Mel's shoulders over the edge and into the crack. Then she heaved upward and shoved the rest of Mel's body over the edge. Mel herself was out of sight now, but Ace was still visible. Frantically, she looked round for a way of climbing up to the crack herself.

The Doctor's brolly!

She grabbed it out of her shoulder bag, and reached upwards with the handle to a protruding spike of ice. She hooked the handle over the spike and tested her weight on it. It held firm. The murderous crewmen and women were just about visible in the gloom. Ace heaved on the brolly and swung her legs upwards. She kicked her feet into the crack, and threw herself over the edge into darkness. She could see the crewmen and women now. She hurriedly grabbed the brolly and pulled her shoulder bag in with her, then crawled down alongside Mel.

The crewmen and women trudged down the Ice Passage – Ace could see them as she peered over the edge. Closer they lurched. Ace held her breath. They'd reached the point where Mel had fallen, and the first one looked down at the fresh blood on the ground. They were only three metres away from her.

'Doctor...' Mel moaned. The first crewman looked round, uncertain. Mel began to move.

Ace put her arm tight round Mel's body. She tried to rock Mel silently – rock her back to sleep.

The crewmen and women shuffled in the passage below. Ace could see the tops of their heads. She held Mel tight in the darkness. Her cheek was pressed against Mel's. She could feel her gentle breathing.

Finally, the crewmen and women lurched on down the passage. Ace watched them as they moved away into the darkness. She listened to their footsteps die away. It seemed to take for ever. When she looked back at Mel's face, Mel had her eyes open.

'What happened?' she asked weakly.

'It's all right, Doughnut,' replied Ace softly in the dark. 'They've gone...'

CHAPTER EIGHT

The Doctor and Glitz found their way blocked by an old
bulkhead door midway down one of the Ice Passages. It
wasn't sealed closed, but it was stiff from many years'
disuse, and the Doctor and Glitz had to heave on it in
unison to prise it open. The passage was darker on the
other side. The Doctor peered through and then
consulted the map. 'I think we go straight on.' He turned
the map round the other way. 'Either that, or . . .' – he
turned the map on its side – 'or. we don't.' Glitz
cautioned the Doctor to be quiet. The Doctor listened.
From the far side of the door, there came a strange sound
– a heavy, rasping sound, like the breathing of some kind
of giant. Glitz edged forward.

Silently, they stepped through the open bulkhead, and
crept down the passage. The rasping sound grew louder.
Glitz pulled out the hand-gun he had taken from Belázs
and continued to edge forward. They reached a side
passage. Glitz peered cautiously round it. There was
nothing there. The strange sound was coming from the
passage opposite. Glitz threw himself round the corner
of the second passage.

Standing directly in front of him was the Creature –
huge and terrifying, like the skeleton of a deformed
monster. Its jaws seemed to glisten like steel razors, as it
reared up and turned on Glitz, and two beams of fire
streaked from its glowing red eyes towards him.

'It's the dragon! Get back!'

Stumbling and slipping, Glitz and the Doctor ran back towards the bulkhead door. The Creature lunged after them, and another two beams of fire pierced the air and burst on the ice just over the Doctor's shoulder. The Doctor and Glitz dived through the bulkhead door.

'Help me close the door, Doctor!'

The Creature was advancing down the passage towards them, as the Doctor and Glitz heaved on the door. Finally, it swung shut, and Glitz pushed the sealing bolts home. Exhausted, he fell back against the door and looked at the Doctor. 'Well, now that we've found the Dragonfire, what's next on the map's list of tourist attractions, Doctor?' But the Doctor's attention was fixed on a lower quarter of the door.

'Ah – I'm not absolutely certain that this one is over yet...'

Glitz followed the Doctor's gaze, and saw a small spot on the door that was beginning to burn through. Quickly, the hole worked its way around the edge of the door.

'Fascinating,' murmured the Doctor. 'It must be generating a spot temperature in excess of 1500 °C.'

Glitz felt a sudden cold chill that was nothing to do with the ice all around – it was the chill of death. He turned to the Doctor for possibly the last time. He would have preferred to die some other way – full of glory – but at least he wouldn't die alone. 'I've never been one for mindless heroic gestures, Doctor. Couldn't see any future in them. But just in case I don't get another opportunity to say this: you're all right by me.'

The Doctor turned to look at Glitz, and was about to say something when Glitz interrupted him. 'Stand back, Doctor.' A neat line of scorched metal ran round the outside edge of the door, and was beginning to splinter as the Creature heaved against it from the other side. Glitz fingered the trigger of his gun. The doorway burst in.

Glitz raised his gun and braced himself. There stood the Creature, in the doorway, right in Glitz's line of fire. He squeezed on the trigger.

'No!' The Doctor grabbed Glitz's arm and pulled it away. Glitz's shot exploded into the wall.

'Doctor!' cried Glitz in terror and amazement. He tried to pull his arm back, but the Doctor held on.

'No, Glitz – don't!'

Glitz waited for the beam of fire that would certainly kill them both. Nothing happened.

The Creature was standing in the doorway, looking at the Doctor and Glitz uncertainly; they were at its mercy, if it wanted to kill them. Instead, the Creature backed away, and lumbered off into the shadows.

Soon, its rasping breath was gone, and the passages were silent again.

Glitz looked at the Doctor. 'Why?'

The Doctor spoke with the quiet conviction of absolute certainty, the certainty of one who has seen all the terrors of the universe. 'Because we don't have the right to kill – ever.'

'But why didn't *it* kill us?'

'Perhaps we'd better ask it ...'

In the Cryogenics Chamber, Belázs was wandering silently amongst the inert figures in their shadowy tubes. Her expression was sombre.

'Can't sleep, Belázs?'

Belázs started, and turned to see Kracauer step out of the shadows. His voice was warm and honeyed. 'Bad dreams again? Or good dreams?'

Belázs didn't reply, but continued to wander amongst the tubes. Then she turned back to Kracauer. 'How old do you think I am, Kracauer?'

Kracauer shrugged. 'Thirty-three ... thirty-four ...'

'And how old do you think I was when I first agreed to join Kane?'

74

Kracauer just shrugged.

Belázs's voice was hard and bitter. 'Sixteen... That was a long time ago.' She held the palm of her hand up to Kracauer. He saw the scar branded deep in her flesh. 'Look at it, Kracauer.'

'The mark of Kane's sovereign.' His voice had turned cold.

'How many years do you think the scar will stay, Kracauer? You'd have thought that after nearly twenty years it would begin to disappear. But no.' She grabbed Kracauer's own arm, and twisted it round, so that he was forced to gaze at his own mark. Her voice was an intense whisper. 'How many years, Kracauer? A whole lifetime?' She let go of his arm and turned away. 'How many years before the mark goes away? Does it *ever* go away?'

Kracauer slowly lowered his arm. 'We sold ourselves. We knew what we were doing. We had a choice.'

'I was *sixteen*!'

'Even at sixteen, we had a choice.'

'And we still have a choice! We can *choose* to leave. He can't own us for ever.'

'People have chosen to leave before. They didn't live long. Death followed them, and caught them up.'

'Only as long as *he* is alive. If he dies, the mark dies with him!'

'His blood temperature is minus 200 °C. Touch one part of his flesh with yours and your living tissue will die. How do you propose to kill him?'

'With heat! Even here in Iceworld, it's too warm for him. I've seen inside the Restricted Zone. It's where he keeps his refrigeration unit. He has to return there whenever his body temperature rises too high. Destroy his refrigeration unit, Kracauer, and he'll die!'

Kracauer saw flames of hatred burning in Belázs's eyes. He smiled.

*

75

Ace had cleaned the large cut on Mel's head, and then produced a small camping fire and some chemicals out of her canvas shoulder bag. The two women now sat in silence, their faces lit by the flickering glow of the flames, Ace intent on her chemical reactions, and Mel watching her. Mel spoke.

'I don't know how to say thank you ...'

Ace felt uncomfortable, and she bit her lip and continued heating liquids.

'You saved my life, Ace.'

'Look, you're putting me off.' Ace's voice sounded slightly annoyed. Why was Mel trying to embarrass her like this?

'Sorry.'

Ace relaxed. Maybe Mel wasn't trying to embarrass her at all. 'Yeah, well ... It all balances out on the end.' She continued mixing chemicals, and her mind wandered back to Perivale. 'Do you know what I did for a job when they threw me out of school?'

'No.'

'I worked as a waitress in a fast-food café. Day in, day out, the same boring routine. The same boring life. It was all wrong. It didn't feel like me that was doing it at all. I felt like I'd fallen from another planet, and landed in this strange girl's body, but it wasn't me at all. I was meant to be somewhere else. Each night, I'd walk home, and I'd look up at the stars through the gaps in the clouds. And I'd try to imagine where I really came from. What my real Mum and Dad were doing. What my real body was doing – not this awkward, clumsy, spotty thing that I was stuck inside. I used to look up at the stars, and dream that one day everything would come right. One day something would come and take me back home. Back to my real home.' She sighed miserably. 'Then it really happened ... and I ended up here. Ended up working as a boring waitress again. Only this time, I couldn't dream of going nowhere else. There wasn't

76

nowhere else to go.' She looked up at Mel, and saw that Mel was smiling. Ace flared up angrily. 'Here – what you laughing for?'

Mel shook her head dreamily. 'Because you just described the way I used to feel five years ago, when I was a teenager. How I still feel, sometimes. How everybody feels sometimes.'

Ace relented, and looked down at the fire. She stared into the dancing flames. 'There's something I've never told anybody. Do you promise not to laugh, and not tell no one?' She looked up at Mel, with large, trusting eyes.

'Never.'

'My name... it's not really Ace. My real name's Dorothy.' She suddenly looked anxious. 'That's how I knew they couldn't be my real Mum and Dad. My *real* Mum and Dad would never have given me a naff name like Dorothy. Don't you see?'

Mel smiled sympathetically.

Ace's anxiety melted away, and she smiled in return. She turned to pack away the chemicals. 'Come on then, Doughnut. Time to move.'

Kane's body was growing warm again, and the atmosphere of Iceworld clung to him oppressively. He returned to his cabinet in the Restricted Zone to cool down again. The statue sparkled with an intoxicating beauty as Kane passed it. He turned to look at it. 'One day, when we return home, I shall erect colossal statues in your honour. The final act of your killers will be to kneel in front of the monuments, and see the past rewritten! I promise you this.'

He turned away from the statue, and lay in his refrigeration cabinet. The lid closed, and the automatic voice began to intone the temperature. 'Ambient cabinet temperature: minus 10 °C. Target temperature: minus 193 °C. Cabinet temperature falling... minus 20 °C... minus 30 °C...' The voice continued as Kane closed his eyes. '... minus 70 °C ... minus 80 °C ...'

A figure emerged from the shadows: Kracauer.

He approached the cabinet, and looked inside. Through the transparent lid, he saw Kane lying dormant inside. A control column stood a few metres away. Kracauer inspected it and located the thermostat controls. He reset them for 30 °C above ice. The voice continued to monitor the temperature, '... minus 175 °C ... minus 180 °C ... minus 185 °C ... minus 185 °C. Steady at minus 185 °C. Ambient cabinet temperature: minus 185 °C and rising ... minus 180 °C ... minus 175 °C ...' But Kane was unconscious, and didn't hear the voice.

Mel and Ace reached a fork in the Ice Passage, and stopped to decide which way to go. 'Down there?' guessed Mel, pointing down one passage.

Ace shrugged. 'I suppose so.'

'Ah, Mel – you've brought my umbrella, I see!'

Mel spun round to see the Doctor striding out of a side passage. 'Doctor!'

'Professor!' cried Ace, with a broad smile. Then her face fell as she saw Glitz following the Doctor. 'Bilgebag,' she sneered.

'Sprog,' countered Glitz.

'No squabbling, now,' interrupted the Doctor, before Ace and Glitz could start fighting. 'There's no place for animosity in a serious scientific undertaking.'

'You mean the dragon?' inquired Mel.

'Actually, it doesn't seem to be a dragon at all,' explained the Doctor. 'It seems to be more of a semi-organic vertebrate with a highly developed cerebral cortex.'

Ace was jumping up and down with excitement. 'And it's got laser beams in its eyes, and it tried to kill us!'

The Doctor turned to Ace. 'Did it really? Hmm, I wonder what you did to annoy it?'

'It just came at us, Professor! No warning!'

'Well, let's see what this vertebrate with laser beams in its eyes has got to say for itself, shall we?' The Doctor strode off down the passage, but after a few steps found his way blocked. He looked up, and found himself staring into the lifeless face of one of the crewmen sent after Mel and Ace. The Doctor raised his hat politely. 'Ah! Hello, and where might you have popped up from, then?'

'Don't argue with it, Doctor,' called Mel. 'Run!'

The Doctor quickly replaced his hat. 'Well, can't stop. My young friend says we should be running along now – and she's usually right in these matters.'

The four companions turned to escape back up the Ice Passage, but a crew-woman lurched out of the first side passage, blocking their escape. The companions turned back, and tried to escape down the second fork of the passage, but another crewman appeared in that exit. They were completely surrounded by the five crewmen and women.

'What do they want with us?' asked the Doctor.

'They've been sent by Kane,' explained Mel.

'He's got masses of them frozen in his deep freeze!' added Ace.

'Cryogenics, eh?' muttered the Doctor, as the crewmen and women began to advance.

Glitz peered at the first crewman. There was something familiar... 'Hang about. I'd recognise this mutinous rabble anywhere!'

'Friends of yours, are they?' asked Ace sarcastically.

Glitz turned to address the murderous zombies. 'Lads, lasses, you won't believe how pleased I am to see you again.' The crewmen and women halted, and turned slowly to look at Glitz. He stepped forward to speak to them. 'Surely you remember me – Glitz? The times we had together. Don't you remember?' The crewmen and women stared blankly at Glitz.

'It's no use, Glitz,' explained the Doctor. 'Ace says they've been cryogenically frozen.'

Glitz ignored the Doctor, and tried to make contact with his former crew. 'Don't you remember that time we bought a load of vegetables cheap, and then discovered they were ferocious biting vegetables from Vega-3!' He turned with feigned concern to one of the crew-women. 'By the way, Winterbottom, how are the bite-marks getting along? Can you manage to sit down now?' There was no movement in the crew-woman's expression.

'It's no use,' the Doctor tried to explain. 'Deep cryogenesis causes sclerosis of the conscious neural pathways.'

'What about that time we captured a space freighter, and then discovered it was carrying natural fruit alcohol? We got well dehydrated that night, eh?' The crewmen and women continued to stare blankly at Glitz, as though they hadn't heard him.

'It's completely impossible for them to recall any events prior to cryogenesis.'

But there was a flicker in the face of the tallest crewman. 'I remember,' he said in a slow, dull voice.

The Doctor turned on the crewman in amazement. 'In fact, there's only one possible exception to this –'

'I remember how you left us behind once on a barren asteroid . . .'

'– and that's in the case of overpowering anger and hatred!'

The overpowering anger and hatred began to force its way into the face of the tall crewman, who turned to look at Glitz with venom. 'I remember how you always got first choice of our pickings.'

Glitz began to get worried. 'Really? I don't recall . . .'

'I remember, I remember how you sold us to Kane, to be frozen as mercenaries.'

'Lads, lasses, come on – a joke's a joke.'

The crewmen and women began to advance on the

four companions with hatred in their eyes.

'I thought they were friends of yours, Bilgebag?'

'Well, more *acquaintances* actually.'

The tall crewman drew his gun, and raised it in front of him. Glitz turned away, not daring to look.

A beam of fire cut through the air.

The gun fell out of the tall crewman's hands. Glitz looked up, to see him slump to the ground. Another beam of fire burst on a second crewman and he fell to the ground, dead.

The companions looked round, and in the darkness behind one of the crew-women, they saw the Creature. The remaining crewman and two crew-women turned with their guns towards the Creature, but it picked them off in quick succession. Then it turned on the companions.

'It's going to kill us!' cried Ace, but the Doctor motioned them all to stand still. The Creature watched them all.

The Doctor stepped forward quite slowly and stood four or five metres in front of the Creature. 'We don't intend to harm you. Can you understand?' Then he slowly put his hand to his head and, with a polite smile, raised his hat. The Creature watched him. The Doctor replaced his hat and then repeated the action. The Creature watched him carefully, then raised its own long, skeletal arm to its skull and tapped the front of its head.

The Doctor turned to the others with a smile. 'You see where a little common courtesy gets you?'

The Creature had taken a few huge strides down the passage, but then stopped and turned back, as though waiting for the others.

'It wants us to go with it, Professor.'

'Well, let's see what our new friend wants to show us, then.'

They set off down the passage, after the Creature.

Glitz looked back for a moment at his dead crew lying on the ground. They could be trouble at times, but they were all right underneath. Poor Winterbottom. He'd never intended this to happen when he sold them to Kane...

'Danger. Approaching defrost threshold. Minus 10 °C and rising... minus 5 °C... 0 °C... Danger. Defrost threshold crossed. Ambient cabinet temperature: 0 °C and rising... plus 1 °C... plus 2 °C... plus 3 °C...'

The lid of the cabinet clicked open automatically. Kane struggled to reach over the side and pull himself upright. His whole body was on fire! He was gasping in the burning air. 'What is happening?' he croaked weakly. 'The cryostat controls... I'm too hot... Can't breathe...' His strength gave way, and he fell to his knees. He knew he had to reach the cryostat controls, and he dragged himself, crawling, across the ground. In front of the cryostat central column stood Kracauer. Kane looked up at him. 'Kracauer... What is this?' He tried to reach up past Kracauer to the controls, but Kracauer didn't move. 'I must, must adjust the cryostat controls...'

Kracauer raised his foot, and pushed Kane backwards with it, laughing. Kane collapsed on the floor again. He crawled around blindly, agonisingly. 'No...' He reached the foot of the statue. The base was swimming in water. Kane felt the water, and realised what it was. He looked up fearfully. The statue was melted beyond all recognition. 'No. Not my statue!'

He began to claw his way up the statue. It took all his strength, all his determination. He forced himself to stand up. Kracauer hadn't expected him to have this much strength.

'Who is responsible for this?' Kane turned to face Kracauer. He needed no support now. He began to step slowly towards Kracauer. 'Who has desecrated the monument? Who? *Who?*' He seized Kracauer by the throat, and began to squeeze.

Kracauer grabbed Kane's arms, and tried to prise them off him, but Kane was driven by blind fury now. 'Who told you? Tell me their name! *Who?*' Tighter and tighter Kane squeezed, squeezing all the breath out of Kracauer, squeezing all the life out of him. Kracauer struggled for breath – but there was none. He thrashed around wildly. Tighter and tighter Kane squeezed, until Kracauer stopped struggling, and fell dead to the ground.

Kane turned to the cryostat column and hit the red emergency button. A flood of refrigerated gases was released from the column, enveloping Kane with refreshing coolness. He steadied himself against the column, as he felt the gases quench the fires in his body. But there was one fire that wouldn't go out – and his eyes were filled with consuming hatred.

'Belázs!'

Belázs was sitting in Kane's seat in the Control Room. She looked at the controls in front of her, and smiled.

'Ah! My dear Belázs.'

She swung round, terrified. It wasn't possible!

Kane approached her from the small door to the Restricted Zone. His face wore a friendly smile. 'You know, I've been thinking... I've been thinking over your request to leave me.'

Belázs didn't dare take her eyes off him for one second. But there was nothing unusual in his expression – except perhaps for the smile, which she hadn't seen since she was a fresh, young teenager. What had Kracauer done in the Restricted Zone? Why hadn't he killed Kane?

'You've been with me a long time now, Belázs. I'm very fond of you. I couldn't bear the idea of losing you. But I've been thinking it over very carefully – and I've decided,' – his unfathomable black eyes locked her gaze tight – 'you may leave me.'

'Lea... leave?'

'Whenever you wish.'

Belázs stood frozen, unable even to think.

'Go, Belázs – in fortune and happiness. Let me shake your hand farewell.'

Belázs didn't understand what was happening. She reached out to shake the hand Kane offered. As soon as she touched his flesh, she realised that he wasn't wearing the protective glove. But it was too late. Kane tightened his grip, and Belázs gasped at the intense, freezing pain which shot up her arm and into her neck. Kane's smile twisted with hatred. 'You traitor! I've been planning my revenge for three thousand years! Do you think that I would let you stand in my way, now that I am so close?'

Belázs felt the agonising cold eating through her head like acid, and fell to her knees. Still Kane held his grip. 'For *three thousand years* I have waited – for revenge on my own people. And *no one* is going to stand in my way!'

The once fresh, young teenager lay dead at his feet.

CHAPTER NINE

The Creature strode through the Ice Passages without hesitating; the others had to struggle to keep up. Occasionally, it would stop and look back, as if checking that they were still behind him, but it never waited long enough for them to catch up and rest. It was already in the chamber of the Singing Trees when the others reached it. The long strings of ice swayed in the cool air currents. Mel and Ace, who had never seen in here before, looked about in wonder.

'This is beautiful,' murmured Mel.

'Here, I can hear singing! Where's it coming from, Professor?'

'Shh. I think it wants us to watch.'

The Creature was standing a few metres to one side of the large crystalline structure that stood in the centre of the chamber. Once the others were all watching it, the Creature turned to face the interlocking formation of crystals. Two beams of fire shone from its eyes and seemed to penetrate right to the heart of the structure. Inside the crystals, the beams split into a thousand streaks of colour as they reflected and refracted throughout the perfect optical system.

'What's it doing, Professor?' whispered Ace.

The thousand beams of light seemed to be concentrating round the centre of the structure, and once they reached a certain intensity, they rose up out of the crystalline formation. It was as though they had physical substance, forming themselves into the image of a regally dressed woman – some kind of elder stateswoman. She seemed to hang in the air over the crystalline structure.

'So that's what all this is for!' murmured the Doctor in admiration. 'It's a polydimensional scanning imager. And our friend the Creature is using *itself* as the energy source.'

The elder stateswoman had started to speak. 'Planetary archives. Criminal history, segment 93-12-03. Two of the most vicious examples of the criminal mentality have been the leaders of the notorious Kane-Xana Gang. Until its demise, this gang carried out systematic violence and extortion, unequalled in its brutality.'

The image changed to a static criminal-record hologram of Kane, but the woman's voice continued. 'In view of the sheer evil of his crimes, Kane is to be exiled from the planet Proamon and never allowed to return. He will be banished to the barren planet of Svartos, which has a permanently frozen dark side on which he can survive.'

The image flickered, and changed into a criminal-record hologram of the woman of the Ice Statue.

'Kane's partner, the woman Xana, killed herself during the final siege of the gang's headquarters, to avoid being arrested and tried for her crimes.'

The Creature's beams of fire disappeared, and the images evaporated. The Creature turned to the others.

'Yes, I think we've heard enough,' muttered the Doctor grimly.

Mel turned to the Doctor. 'That explains about Kane. But where does the Creature come from?'

'And what about the treasure?' asked Glitz looking at the fabulous crystalline structure. 'Is this it?'

The Doctor frowned. 'No. We may be deep beneath Iceworld now, but Kane could find this easily enough if he wanted to. No, the real treasure must be somewhere else. Somewhere beyond Kane's reach. What does Kane fear most?'

'Heat. It'll kill him, Professor.'

'Precisely. So what better way of protecting the real treasure than to leave a fire-breathing dragon to guard it? In fact, what better protection than if the dragon *is* the treasure?'

Mel's mouth dropped in wonder. 'The Creature, the treasure?'

The Doctor turned to look at the Creature. Towering over them, with its membranous skin stretched tight over the deformed skeleton, the Creature shuffled slightly.

'Am I right?' asked the Doctor of the Creature. 'Is it *you* that everyone has been looking for?'

As they watched it with a mixture of fascination and revulsion, the membranous sheath covering the Creature's grotesque head began to pull down, revealing the glistening, mucus-covered skull beneath. The skull itself seemed to glitter as though made out of metal. Then it started to expand and break apart. The different segments folded back to reveal, inside the Creature's skull, a huge crystal, crackling with an electric storm that was trapped inside the crystalline lattice.

'It's beautiful,' murmured Ace.

'It's worth a fortune,' murmured Glitz.

'More than that, Glitz,' said the Doctor. 'Look past the fabulously valuable crystal. Look at the fire inside it. A source of intense optical energy. Now look at it through Kane's eyes. See it as an evil mind would see it . . .'

In his Control Room, Kane listened to the Doctor's words via the radio tracking device in the seal of Glitz's map.

'At last,' he whispered to himself, 'after three thousand years, the Dragonfire shall be *mine*!'

In the chamber of the Singing Trees, Glitz smiled. 'I

think I'm beginning to feel a warm, cosy sensation in my money pouch!'

Ace turned angrily on Glitz. 'Lay one finger on the Creature, Bilgebag, and I'll rivet your kneecaps together!'

'All right! Don't get so fidgety, Sprog.'

'Look!' Mel pointed at the Creature. The sections of its skull were hinging back into place, and the membrane skin glided back over the slimy mucus.

Ace screwed her face up in disgust. 'Ugh! That's sick!'

The Doctor wasn't paying attention. He was pacing distractedly, murmuring to himself. 'There's something wrong here. Can't quite put my finger ... Proamon ...'

'The woman in the hologram said that Proamon was Kane's home planet,' volunteered Mel.

'But why have I heard of it before? Where is it? And was it in the past, or is it in the future?'

'Is this really important, Doctor?' complained Glitz.

'Is a grain of sand important, Glitz? I think I'd like to consult the starcharts back in the TARDIS.'

Ace's eyes lit up. 'Your spacecraft? Brill!'

'Doctor, we don't have time,' reminded Mel.

Ace turned on Mel in disbelief. 'Doughnut!'

'No need to perambulate all the way back to Iceworld, Doctor,' interrupted Glitz. 'These passages have got their own star charts. The Ice Garden. I found it, remember?'

The Doctor looked at Glitz. 'A primitive star chart, eh? Basic constellations and orbital calculations, I imagine. It'll be enough for what I want to check.'

Ace's eyes lit up again. 'Ice Garden?'

The Doctor turned to her. 'No, I'd prefer you to stay here. Won't be long.'

Ace's face fell.

'The Doctor's right, Sprog. Very risky enterprise. You two wait here until the Doctor and I get back.'

'Bilgebag!'

The Doctor interrupted before it came to blows. 'Now, now. I'd like you to stay here too, Glitz.'

'Behave, Doctor! I'm not going to nanny these two!'

'Actually, I was thinking they might keep *you* out of trouble. Won't be long.'

Ace stuck her tongue out at Glitz in victory.

CHAPTER TEN

In the Duty Guards' Room Sergeant McLuhan was lying back on one of the bunks. It was the waiting she didn't like. Always waiting. Mostly, just waiting for the end of the shift. Waiting and hoping that something exciting would happen – anything to break the boredom. The most that usually happened was that a fight would break out in the Refreshment Bar and the Duty Guards would be summoned to deal with it. Or somebody would be caught trying to steal goods from the Freezer Centre. Not exactly what McLuhan had had in mind ten years ago when she was going through basic military training as a new recruit. But at least this was work. And at least there was always the possibility that eventually she might get to do some real fighting – fire a weapon somewhere more than just the practice range.

She listened to Bazin on the bunk below as he turned a page in the book he was reading. Why had they teamed her with him? Was it somebody's idea of a joke to give her a partner who hardly seemed to know which end of a gun the pulse beam came out of? Some joke. What would happen if they ever got into danger? Would she be able to rely on Bazin to cover her back? Or would he turn chicken and run, leaving them both to get killed?

She heard him turn another page. She knew what he was reading. The Rule Book. He was always reading the Rule Book. Always quoting it at her. If she could have her way with his Rule Book, he'd never again be able to sit and swallow at the same time!

An undulating whine cut through the boredom, and an amber light began to flash on the communication panel. *What this time?* wondered McLuhan, as Bazin leapt from his bunk beneath her. *Another brawl? Another shoplifter?*

Bazin pressed on the flashing amber light, and replied: 'Duty guards.'

The quiet, sinister voice of Kane hissed softly back out of the intercom. 'We have an incident in the Lower Sectors, Quadrant 6. An aggressive non-terrestrial.'

McLuhan felt a small spark of excitement shoot through her nervous system.

Kane's voice continued. 'It's marked with a radio tracking device. I want the creature eliminated.' There was a slight pause, as though Kane were thinking. 'Bring me back its head.'

The intercom went dead.

McLuhan smiled. *An ANT hunt!*

She swung her legs over the side of the bunk and jumped down. Bazin was checking his hand-gun in readiness. He fumbled with it nervously. McLuhan looked at him sceptically. 'How many ANT-hunts you been on?' she asked.

Bazin looked up, uncertain. 'ANT-hunts?'

'A-N-T: Aggressive Non-Terrestrial,' she explained patiently. 'You ever seen one?'

'Well, not as such . . .'

He'd probably once seen a picture of some brightly coloured creature in a comic book!

'Didn't think so,' sighed McLuhan.

'But it's a standard procedure.'

McLuhan narrowed her eyes. 'What do you think a *standard* non-terrestrial looks like?'

'Well . . .'

'Try thinking of a scorpion, two metres high, coming

at you out of the shadows...'

Bazin's eyes were wide with disbelief and fear. McLuhan picked the hand-gun out of his hands. 'So do me a favour and leave the water pistol at home.' She dropped the hand-gun on one side, and turned to the armoury racks. The Cosmolite .65 gigawatt bolt-beam Heavy Combat Gun weighed ten kilos. Most of that was accounted for by a bolt-beam generator which, at full power, could blow a fifty-centimetre hole in one-metre thick armour plating from two hundred metres distance. 'If I'm relying on you to watch my back, I want to know that you're carrying enough artillery to blow this ANT clean across the Space Lanes.'

She tossed a Cosmolite to Bazin as though it were no heavier than a child's toy. It almost flattened him when he caught it.

In the chamber of the Singing Trees, no one had spoken since the Doctor and the Creature had left. The distant voices sang softly in the breeze, and Glitz, Mel and Ace, each sitting on boulders of ice, drifted along on their own thoughts. Eventually, Glitz sighed, 'This is the life, eh? A whole universe out there, with all the myriad mysteries of the cosmos, and we're sat twiddling our digits in some benighted wodge of permafrost!'

Mel looked up. 'We could always pass the time playing a game, I suppose. *I Spy* or something.'

Ace and Glitz both turned to stare at her.

'Just a suggestion,' offered Mel, lamely.

'Bilgebag's right,' admitted Ace grudgingly. 'I wanted some adventure. I wanted to do something exciting, see something beautiful, just once in my life...'

Glitz smiled. 'You know, believe it or not, I was young once.'

'So was I...' sighed Ace.

'I was a right tearaway,' continued Glitz. 'Thought I knew it all.'

'Some things never change, do they?' taunted Ace.

'Ah-ah,' admonished Glitz, 'allow an old man his moment of pregnant introspection. Where was I?'

'Pregnant introspection,' reminded Mel. 'A right tearaway. Some things never change.'

Glitz recovered the line back through his memories. 'Ah, yes – the things I've seen... The places I've been... Me and the Good Ship *Nosferatu* – been everywhere together. Riding on the Space Winds... Diving through the Rainbow Clouds... Nowhere to go but onwards... The Asteroid Breaks. The Nebula Ridges. Out beyond the edge of the Twelve Galaxies.'

Ace had been listening to this with growing enchantment and was now staring at him wide-eyed. 'You've been outside the Twelve Galaxies?'

'Me and the *Nosferatu*. Been everywhere together.' He sighed. 'The most exquisite delights the universe has to offer. If only I could have bottled them, I'd have myself a nice little earner.'

In the Duty Guards' Room, McLuhan and Bazin stripped down the mechanisms of their Cosmolites, to check one final time that the vibration absorbers were loose and the electrical contacts secure. McLuhan was relieved to see that Bazin's familiarity with the weapon was faultless. She was beginning to feel the effects of the adrenalin in her bloodstream – a sharp fear that tightened her muscles and made her heart race. She looked at Bazin briefly, and wondered how much fear he was hiding and trying not to let her see. He was only a boy really. What was he doing, wasting his life as a soldier?

He snapped the locking bolt into position on his weapon, and looked up. McLuhan snapped her bolt into position, and looked back at him. 'Ready?' she asked.

'Two metres tall, you say?'

'Minimum.' McLuhan's gaze was steady. 'Let's go.'

She saw the fear in the boy's eyes.

If the Doctor had known that the map he was carrying contained a radio tracking device, he would not have been peering at it and muttering, 'They always mark North and South on these things, but never Forwards and Backwards,' as he and the Creature made their way through the dark Ice Passages.

If he had known that the tracking device would lead McLuhan and Bazin to the Creature, he would never have looked up and said, 'Tell you what, you seem to know the way, why don't I leave it to you?'

If he had known that the map would eventually cause the death of the Creature, he would never have tucked it into a fold of the Creature's membranous skin.

If he had known. But he didn't.

CHAPTER ELEVEN

Kane looked down across the Cryogenics Chamber in triumph. From his high gantry, he could see hundreds of dead-faced mercenaries, lined up and waiting for his command. This is what it would be like when he returned to Proamon! His eyes blazed jet-black.

He waited for the final few cryogenics tubes to rise and release their occupants. He had waited three thousand years. He could wait a few moments more. The remaining mercenaries stumbled forward out of their tubes, and took their places in the rows of lifeless, death-filled faces. Kane looked down again and was filled with the exquisite feeling of absolute power.

His voice echoed through the chill silence. 'The time is at hand! In a few hours, when the Dragonfire is finally mine, we shall be able to leave this worthless planet. But first we must clear out all the humans. I want you to spread terror throughout the Upper Levels, and drive the humans towards the Docking Bays. Drive them onto the spacecraft. I want no one left alive in Iceworld. The terror which will seize the planet of Svartos here today, will soon strike the planet of Proamon, my former home. Then we shall move swiftly throughout the whole of the Twelve Galaxies, and take our revenge for the injustices that have been done to us. Once, I was driven from my home; soon, no one in the Twelve Galaxies shall have a home!'

Kane was in total control now, and his final cries rang through the chamber: 'Now go and destroy the humans in Iceworld! The Dragonfire is mine!'

The taste of power was sweet and subtle, like a rare, intoxicating fruit. Kane needed no other food.

The Space Trading Colony of Iceworld usually had between 1,000 and 1,500 travellers in it at any one time, and there were Docking Bays for up to 500 spacecraft. The travellers would stay two or maybe three days, stocking up on food supplies, repairing their spacecraft, or just relieving the boredom of space travel by relaxing in the Refreshment Bar, Sports Hall, Beauty Salon or Restaurant.

Stellar's mother had decided to treat Stellar to a meal in the Restaurant. Well, actually, it wasn't exactly that she wanted to *treat* the little girl – more, that she wanted to treat *herself*, after her traumatic experience with the hooligan waitress and a milkshake – and there wasn't much she could do with Stellar apart from take her along.

Stellar was quite excited to be eating in a grown-ups' restaurant for the first time, and she couldn't wait to get back home and tell her best friend, Milli-mind. The waiters had brought special child-size knives and forks, because the ordinary ones were too big for Stellar. The waitresses had brought some extra cushions for Stellar to sit on, because the chair was too low for small children. They had even brought extra cushions for Ted, Stellar's teddy bear, so that he could sit next to her and watch.

Her mother (now wearing a white, sparkly number fringed with willowy, pink feathers, since the distressing incident with the milkshake) occasionally pointed out famous people as they came and went. That man was the man from Stellar's favourite holovision programme. That man used to be a famous pop vocalist when Stellar's mother was a teenager, and she'd bought all his videos.

That woman was a brilliant scientist, and people said she was the kindest person in the Twelve Galaxies. That woman looks a bit like ... no ... (But Stellar saw that the woman looked a bit, but not exactly, like the woman her father was now living with.)

Stellar would have so much to tell Milli-mind when she got back home!

McLuhan descended the service shaft with only a couple of strides and immediately spun round with the Cosmolite. The first nervous excitement of starting out on the ANT-hunt had now given way to an alert concentration, with the knowledge that she soon might die. She scanned the darkness of the Ice Passage. It seemed to be clear. She nodded up to Bazin, at the top of the ladder, who quickly scrambled down and joined her. They both looked round in the gloom. Their fingers were tight on the triggers of their Cosmolites, balanced lightly on gyroclamps attached to their shoulder harnesses.

'It could be anywhere,' said Bazin. 'How are we going to see it in this dark?'

'Here, use this.' McLuhan passed a small electronic device to Bazin.

'What is it?'

'It's the signal tracker. Kane said the ANT was marked. Tape the tracker on top of your Cosmolite where you can see it. If this ANT so much as twitches, I want to know about it.'

The Doctor had to scramble to keep up with the Creature. It had no hesitation about which way to go, and its tall, skeletal body was perfectly suited to striding over the ice boulders. It took the Doctor straight to the Ice Garden – the huge, domed chamber where tiny flowers sparkled like constellations in the night sky. The Doctor gazed around, breathtaken by the immense beauty of it.

'With silver bells and cockleshells...' he murmured, half-remembering an old Earth nursery rhyme. 'It's magnificent. A huge planetarium.' He peered more closely at the patterns, as though something were wrong. 'But the perspective's distorted. Where was it drawn from? Not here on Svartos. Where is Proamon?'

The Creature gestured with its long, bony arm, and pointed to a slightly raised section in the centre of the floor. In the middle of this area, a single ice flower glittered red. Other smaller white flowers were dotted on circular orbits around it. And at the very rim of the raised section, lay a small, pale-blue flower.

'A solar system. This must be a large red star,' said the Doctor, pointing at the sparkle of red, 'with smaller orbiting planets, and this small blue one must be Proamon.' He looked back at the star-studded roof. 'And these are the constellations seen from out past the Seventh Galaxy: the Waterfall, the Great Lever... but they're not quite right. The shapes are slightly distorted. It's all out of alignment.'

He shook his head. 'It's beautiful, but it's out of date. The star systems have changed. These star charts are no use any longer.' He looked at the Creature, who was watching him. 'How long have you been on this planet? Two thousand years? Longer?'

But the Creature couldn't answer.

'We'd better go back to the others.'

Mel, Ace and Glitz were still sitting glumly in the chamber of the Singing Trees. No one had kept track of how long they had been waiting for the Doctor and the Creature to return – it had been ages. Ace sighed.

'This is naff. This is mega-naff.' She picked up her canvas shoulder-bag and tipped the contents out onto the ground. She poked through the assorted bits and pieces. 'And what's more, I've run out of nitro.' Then she thought of something, and her face brightened. 'But

I've got tons more back in my quarters.'

Mel looked up, her eyes sparkling. 'Let's go back and get it.'

'No, thank you,' interrupted Glitz, 'we'll steer clear of the home-made stuff, I think. There's six hundred kilos of commercial back on board the *Nosferatu*. I'll go and fetch some of that.'

Ace's eyes lit up at the mention of Glitz's spacecraft. 'The *Nosferatu*?'

'And you both stay here,' ordered Glitz, imagining all the trouble he might have with these two.

'Aww . . .' complained Ace loudly.

Glitz turned to her with strained patience. 'Just for once, Sprog, do you think you could do what you're told?'

Ace sat down in a sulk.

'Why do we girls always get left out?' moaned Mel.

Glitz was about to tell her, but decided not to. He always had trouble with feminists – usually because they were right and he was wrong. Instead, he just said, 'I'll be as quick as I can,' and he disappeared down one of the Ice Passages.

Mel and Ace sat glumly.

The crunch of Glitz's footsteps on the ice disappeared down the passage.

Slowly, the two women turned to each other. A broad smile broke out on both their faces. They stood up, and crept quietly after Glitz. Ace peered cautiously round the corner of the passage. No one in sight! Quickly, they scampered down the passage, following Glitz's tracks in the snow. The tracks turned into a side passage further along. Ace crept up, with Mel close behind her. Together, they peered round the corner.

'Yeek!' they both shrieked in unison, as they suddenly came face to face with a cross-looking Glitz staring back at them and growling.

'Grrr!'

Glitz didn't look to be in any mood for discussions, so Mel and Ace scurried back to the chamber. They sat down in a sulk once more.

Ace sighed.

'I spy, with my little eye, something beginning with *I*.' Her voice was dull and bored.

'Ice,' said Mel, equally bored.

'Your go.'

McLuhan and Bazin had been following the tracking signal for almost an hour. It had been growing steadily stronger, and they had now almost caught up with their foe. McLuhan knew that nothing they had been taught in training would be of use to them now. No amount of preparation could replace fast reactions, perfect aim, and telepathic teamwork. And no rule book could replace the tight fear that held her body tense and alert.

She also knew the one rule that wasn't written in any rule book: average life expectancy on an ANT-hunt is one hour fifty-three minutes. The longer the hunt goes on, the more likely the alien is to win. And the losers never returned home. She wondered whether Bazin knew that rule as well – whether he was counting the minutes as well.

'It's here!' he hissed. The tracker was registering a strong signal.

'Where?'

'About fifty metres, straight ahead.'

Without thinking, McLuhan checked the mechanism on her Cosmolite, and then tightened her finger on the trigger. They moved cautiously ahead, Bazin concentrating on the tracker, McLuhan staring down the passage ahead. She couldn't see anything.

'There's nothing there!'

'It's there. Forty metres now – slightly to the right.'

McLuhan peered down the passage. About ten metres ahead, another passage forked off to the right.

'Thirty metres. Coming towards us . . .'

'It's that passage ahead! Ready to open fire!'

Silently, McLuhan and Bazin both dropped down to a kneeling position and flicked up the sights on their Cosmolites.

'Twenty metres!' hissed Bazin.

Carefully, McLuhan lined her sights up on the point where she expected the alien to appear. Her breathing slowed down to calm, measured breaths, and her finger began to depress the trigger until she felt the slight resistance of its trigger point.

'Ten!'

Then she saw it! A terrifying alien skeleton with angry red eyes!

At the same instant, a bolt-beam from Bazin's Cosmolite burst into the wall of the Ice Passage just in front of the alien. He'd fired too soon – and missed!

McLuhan pulled her finger, but it was too late now; the alien had disappeared from the centre of her gunsight. She saw her own bolt-beam explode into the opening of the second passage at the same time as she saw two streaks of fire beam out of the alien's eyes. Without thinking, she rolled away, and felt one of the beams scorch her arm as it hit the ground where she had been lying. She fired half a dozen more bolt-beams down the passage, just hoping that one of them might hit its target. In her confusion, she saw another figure down the passage – a human. She didn't know whether or not she hit the figure or the alien with any of her volley of shots. But she knew that she was vulnerable lying on the ground and had to get up. Another volley of bolt-beams, from Bazin's Cosmolite, exploded down the passage as McLuhan scrambled to her feet. The passage was empty ahead of her. No alien, no human, no bodies. 'Where is it?' she hissed.

Bazin glanced at the signal tracker. 'To the left. Sixty metres. Moving away.'

'Come on! Don't lose the signal!'

She hurried down the passage, but she knew that they had wasted their best opportunity. They had lost the element of surprise. One hour fifty-three minutes was an average: some people lasted longer – but that meant that others died sooner . . .

CHAPTER TWELVE

Stellar and her mother had almost finished their meal. Despite unfortunate recent experiences, her mother had allowed Stellar to have ice cream for dessert, which Stellar had declared to be 'Fantastick!' Now she was just waiting for her mother to finish her decaffeinated and they would be ready to leave.

A passing waiter brushed against the chair that Ted was sitting on and knocked it. Stellar's teddy bear rolled forward, bounced lightly on the edge of the table, and then disappeared underneath.

'Pick him up, darling, or you'll lose him,' said her mother. So Stellar slipped down off her cushions and onto the floor. She peered under the table, and could just see Ted on the other side.

At the same moment, the door to the Restaurant burst violently open. Startled diners looked up to see twenty or more living corpses – Kane's frozen mercenaries – stagger in. A woman's scream was the trigger for general terror, as diners leapt from their meals in confusion and panic, and tried to fight their way out of the Restaurant.

Stellar, under the table, heard the screaming, and saw the legs of people running past, kicking chairs in all directions. Her mother tried to reach down and rescue Stellar, but the chaotic rush of frightened people carried the woman away and towards the exits. 'My daughter! Let me get my daughter!' she screamed, but nobody heard her, and she was jostled away.

An old woman, who couldn't run as fast as the others, snapped like an autumn twig. A man who bravely tried to help her, fell broken alongside her. The empty-faced killers were unstoppable.

Stellar couldn't see what was happening, and was puzzled by all the commotion. She decided she had better sit where she was until her mother told her what to do.

The mercenaries' instructions had been to create terror, and drive everyone towards the Docking Bays. Their orders were to leave no one alive in Iceworld. They looked around the Restaurant now and saw no one left alive. Most of the diners had fled, only to find themselves driven towards the Docking Bays by other mercenaries. The few who hadn't run, or hadn't run fast enough, were lying dead on the floor.

Stellar didn't understand why her mother had left her behind. She looked around from under the table. A tall, horrible-looking man was stumbling towards her. She sat still under the table. She saw his strong legs stagger up to her table. He stood right over Ted, with one foot either side of the toy.

The mercenary was unsure; it thought it could sense a living creature close by, but it couldn't see anything. From beneath the table, a small arm emerged. The mercenary shuffled. Its feet brushed against a child's plaything on the ground. It looked at the dead bodies on the floor. The small arm pulled at the teddy bear between the mercenary's feet, but it was standing on one of the toy's ears. The mercenary looked round and shuffled again. The small arm pulled the teddy free, and took it under the table. The mercenary looked at the ground where it stood, but saw nothing there. Then it stumbled off after its colleagues.

The Restaurant was silent.

Stellar looked round from under the table. She

couldn't see anybody. Carefully, she crept out, bringing
Ted with her. She stood up.

Chairs were lying broken. Plates and dishes were
smashed on the floor. An old woman and a man were
lying asleep in the most uncomfortable positions. Food
was spilt everywhere.

'Naughty Ted! Look what's happened, all because
you jumped under the table.'

The refrigeration cabinet stood waiting as Kane strode
into the Restricted Zone. He needed time alone – time to
prepare himself. After three thousand years of waiting,
he needed to concentrate his mind.

He lay down inside the cabinet, folded his arms across
his chest, and closed his eyes. With a slight hiss, the lid of
the cabinet closed and sealed itself shut. Refrigerating
gases began to fill the cabinet.

'Current cabinet temperature: minus 15 °C ... Target
cabinet temperature: minus 193 °C ... Cabinet temperature falling ... minus 20 °C ... minus 30 °C ... minus
40 °C ...'

This would be the last time that Kane would ever need
to refresh his body temperature here on Svartos.

The customers in Iceworld fled from the relentless
mercenaries like terrified animals. They were used to
living civilised lives on civilised planets. If any kind of
disaster threatened, they had leaders to guide them – that
was why they elected governments and leaders in the
first place. Now they found themselves without leaders
to tell them what to do, and they were terrified. After a
lifetime of relying on other people to make their
decisions, and of doing what they were told, they had lost
the ability to think clearly in an emergency. They were
easy prey for the empty-faced men and women.

The mercenaries herded them like senseless sheep.
They drove them from the Freezer Centre, from the

Refreshment Bar, and from the Sports Hall. They stampeded them down corridors, and gradually herded the panic-stricken people towards the Docking Bays, as Kane had ordered.

Stellar knew nothing of this. The mercenaries had missed her, and left her behind. She trailed through the empty corridors with her teddy, wondering where everyone was, and why her mother had left her. There was no one about. No muzak drifting from the loudspeakers. No cheery announcements from the *Bing-bong* Woman. Nothing.

Stellar supposed she would have to find her own way back to the spacecraft, but she wasn't sure which way to go. She looked at the signs on the walls, as she had seen her mother do when she wanted directions, but Stellar hadn't learned to read yet, and the signs had arrows pointing in every direction.

She remembered that they had come up in a lift from the spacecraft, so when she saw a sign pointing down a service shaft, she decided that it must be the right way to get back to the spacecraft. She smiled, and thought of how surprised her mother was going to be when she discovered that Stellar had found her way back all by herself.

But when she got to the bottom of the ladder, she wasn't at all sure that this was the right way after all. It was darker down here, and instead of tidy corridors, the way was along metal walkways with ice walls. There was another passage off to one side, so Stellar decided to look down there. But it was the same as the first one. She turned back to return up the service shaft to where she had started. But she must have taken an extra turning somewhere, because she couldn't find the ladder again. She wandered further down the Ice Passages, moving deeper beneath Iceworld, and hoping that she could find some way back to her mother.

'Naughty Ted. It was your idea to come this way, and

now you've got us lost.'

The Doctor didn't know whether the Creature was still alive, or dead. They had been ambushed by two of Kane's guards, and the Doctor had been lucky to escape with his life. But in the confusion, the Creature had disappeared in a different direction.

He hurried back to the chamber of the Singing Trees to collect Mel, Ace and Glitz, but when he arrived, Glitz wasn't there – only the two women sitting glumly. Mel was the first to see the Doctor, and she jumped up. 'Doctor!'

'That doesn't begin with *M*,' complained Ace, who still hadn't noticed the Doctor.

'Where's Glitz?' demanded the Doctor.

Ace spun round in delight. 'Professor!'

'He's gone back to his spacecraft,' answered Mel.

The Doctor turned to go. 'Come on, hurry! Time is only skin deep, and the Creature's in terrible danger. We've got to stop Kane!'

He strode off, and the two women hurried after him.

McLuhan and Bazin had been tracking the Creature for an hour and a half, and were now making their way along the metal gantries directly beneath the Staff Quarters. McLuhan didn't believe the signal tracker as it led them further upwards towards Iceworld, but Bazin insisted that the signal was growing stronger.

'We're too close to the Upper Levels,' she hissed.

Bazin was intent on the tracker. 'It's here!'

McLuhan felt a sudden tightening of her stomach. She swiftly peered round the surrounding passage. There was nothing. 'Where?'

Bazin scanned the area with the signal tracker. 'I don't understand...'

'Where is it?'

'It's everywhere.'

'What do you mean – *everywhere*?'

'I don't know. Whichever direction I point the signal tracker, I get the same reading.'

'I told you it was giving a false reading.'

'No, it's here somewhere. It's coming towards us!'

McLuhan stared frantically round. There was nothing in sight. 'It's wrong. There's nothing here.'

'Still approaching. Fifteen metres.'

'There's nothing there, Bazin! The tracker's wrong!' But she knew it wasn't.

'Ten metres...'

McLuhan swung round wildly. 'Where is it?' she screamed in panic.

'It's all around us! Five metres...'

'*Where*, for God's sake?'

'It's here! It's here somewhere!'

'*Where?*'

They both looked frantically round. There was nothing in either direction down the passage. Suddenly, they heard a scraping sound from beneath the metal walkway they were standing on. 'It's down there!' shouted Bazin, and immediately began to open fire at the metal gantry. The bolt-beams blew a large section of the gantry away, along with the ice beneath.

A child screamed!

'Stop!' shouted McLuhan. 'Hold your fire!' She pulled Bazin's hand away from the trigger of his Cosmolite.

The burnt metal of the gantry still crackled from the heat, and hot pieces of metal hissed as they fell into the melted ice. A small girl was crying fearfully. McLuhan covered the source of the sound with her own Cosmolite. 'Come out!' she ordered.

Slowly, the frightened Stellar crawled out through a gap at the side of the walkway.

'It's a girl,' said Bazin, still confused.

'Come on – right up here.'

Stellar climbed up onto the walkway, pulling her teddy with her.

'But . . . how come the tracker's picking *her* up?'

It wasn't. The Creature dropped down out of the metalwork in the roof of the passage. Stellar screamed when she saw the terrifying alien. Without even seeing the Creature, McLuhan and Bazin both knew what was behind them. They spun round with their Cosmolites. But they knew the Creature had the advantage this time.

Bazin felt no pain at first. That came later. He simply felt his shoulder wrenched violently backwards, as the streak of fire from the Creature's eyes impacted. It spun him sideways and he fell to his knees.

McLuhan didn't even think. She threw her arm round Bazin's body and dragged him to his feet. Without breaking the movement, she hauled him down a side passage. By the time she realised what was happening, they were two passages away, and beyond the Creature's range.

The Creature didn't follow the two who escaped. It stared at the small human who didn't run away.

Stellar was terrified. She hugged Ted close to her, in fear. The Creature was like something out of one of the small girl's nightmares – the terrible, disfigured monsters that made her scream out in the night.

The Creature heard the small child's whimpers. It didn't understand language, but it could recognise the meaning of sounds. This was the sound of fear. It reached out slowly towards the child.

Stellar recoiled in terror.

The Creature paused, and waited. Then it reached out again, very slowly, so that it didn't frighten the child. Its bony arm reached forward, and it extended a long finger to touch the toy which the child was clutching.

Stellar flinched slightly, but then she saw that the Creature only wanted to touch Ted. Perhaps the Creature wasn't going to hurt her at all. Slowly, she held

109

Ted out for the Creature to see. The Creature ran its finger lightly over Ted's ears. A smile broke through Stellar's anxiety, and spread across her face.

The Creature recognised that the small child was no longer frightened. It reached out its bony finger again, and ran it over the child's hair.

Stellar felt the Creature's light touch, and she knew that it wouldn't hurt her. It looked frightening at first, but it was friendly underneath. She reached out towards it and touched its membranous skin. It felt softer than anything she'd ever felt before. It felt like a fluffy, white cloud must feel – if you could stroke a cloud. Or a rainbow. Or a dream.

The Creature reached forward with both arms and lifted the child up. She didn't mind. She wasn't scared now. She nestled in the soft folds of its skin as it carried her away down the passage.

Mel and Ace scrambled over the ice to keep up with the Doctor.

'Slow down, Doctor!'

'No time, Mel.'

'But where are we going?' moaned Ace from a few metres behind the others.

'Back to the TARDIS.'

Ace's eyes lit up. 'Your spacecraft!'

'But what about the Creature?' insisted Mel. 'We've got to save it.'

'The Creature's always going to be in danger from Kane. The only way we can save it is by convincing Kane that his star charts are hopelessly wrong. If we can do that, we might be able to stop all this.'

The Doctor strode on ahead. Ace hurried to catch up with Mel. 'Here – this isn't another wind-up is it? I mean, I really am going to see your spacecraft this time, aren't I?'

'Who knows?' sighed Mel.

★

For three thousand years, the Creature had lived almost entirely in the Lower Levels, beyond Kane's reach. It avoided the humans in the Upper Levels, but it still remembered every twist and turn in the Ice Passages that led up to Iceworld.

Stellar was asleep in the Creature's soft embrace as it strode silently through the deserted corridors. Her nose twitched occasionally in her dreams.

The Creature reached the Refreshment Bar, and gently laid Stellar down in a chair. It recognised her soft, contented breathing. Then it turned to go.

It looked back once before leaving her.

It wouldn't see her alive again.

'Most ingenious,' remarked the Doctor when he saw the climbing ropes that Mel and Ace had used to get down the Ice Face. 'These should save us some time.'

He insisted that Mel went first, with him and Ace pulling on the free end. Then Ace followed, with the Doctor pulling from beneath, and Mel helping from above. And finally, the Doctor himself went, with the two women heaving from above.

'Not too heavy for you, was I?' asked the Doctor when he reached the top. Mel decided not to bother telling him about the problems they had had with the nitro on the way down, and how she had had to struggle one-handed to rescue Ace. She didn't want to worry the Doctor ...

Stellar woke up and looked round a bit sleepily. She had had the strangest dream – about a snow world and a terrible creature that turned out to be soft and friendly.

Where was everyone? And where was her mother? Then she remembered – about hiding under the table while all the grown-ups ran past shouting. She remembered that she and Ted were on their way back to the spacecraft.

She slid down from the chair and rubbed the sleep out

of her eyes. She noticed a glass of starfruit milkshake standing on the bar. None of it had been drunk. It must have been left behind when everyone ran away.

She pulled a tall bar-stool over, and clambered up onto it. The ice cream in the milkshake had melted – and Stellar giggled when she remembered what the waitress had done to her mother with a milkshake.

Once she had finished the milkshake, Stellar slithered down off the bar-stool, and trotted off out of the Refreshment Bar in search of the spacecraft. She'd already forgotten her dream.

CHAPTER THIRTEEN

McLuhan hauled Bazin down passage after passage until her legs ached. Then she lowered him to the ground, and sank down beside him.

'Morphine . . .' gasped Bazin, his face contorted with pain. 'I need morphine . . .'

'No you don't,' reassured McLuhan. 'You can do it without morphine.' She knew what would happen if she gave him a shot of morphine. It would kill the pain, but it would also leave him floating through a haze of drug-induced psychedelia. And she wanted him awake and alert, or else they would both be dead.

The Creature was following them, she was certain of that. It all depended on how soon it caught up with them. If she had time to fix Bazin up somehow, they might still have a chance.

She turned to look at Bazin's injury. It was bad. His left shoulder was burnt away. No wonder the boy was asking for morphine.

Obviously it would need extensive surgery to do the job properly, and even that might not save Bazin's left arm, but McLuhan just wanted to patch it up enough to make him some use to her.

'I think I'm going to throw up,' warned Bazin.

'It's shock,' she advised him. 'It'll pass.' She could see the sweat pouring down his pale face, and she felt at his brow. It was ice-cold. She had to do something to stop him going into major post-injury trauma – the PITs, as it was called by those who survived.

He turned to one side and tried to throw up, but all he could do was retch violently.

'That's good,' she said. 'Get it out of your system.' When he had recovered, she wiped his face with her sleeve. Then, she unclamped both of their Cosmolites, and took off both their shoulder harnesses. She took her own belt off, looping it round Bazin's neck, to form a make-shift sling. Then she took her combat jacket off. It was chilly in the Ice Passages, but she had to keep Bazin warm if he was to keep going. She hooked his injured arm in the belt looped round his neck. Then she pushed his good arm into the sleeve of her jacket, and wrapped the rest of it round his shoulders and over his injured arm, fastening it at the front.

She slipped her shoulder harness back on, and clamped her Cosmolite back into position. She took the signal tracker from Bazin's Cosmolite, but left his gun lying on the ground.

'Can you walk?'

'I'll try.'

He'd lost a lot of strength, owing to the shock, but McLuhan knew that it would return once they got going. She helped him to his feet. 'Come on, we're not safe here. We've got to keep moving.'

With his good arm round her shoulder for support, Bazin started to stumble down the passageway. McLuhan admired the boy's courage, the way he was fighting the pain. He was badly crippled by the injury, but even a cripple would be better than no one when the time finally came to face the Creature.

A cold breeze blew among the hundreds of empty tubes in the Cryogenics Chamber. The atmosphere was even more chill and eerie than before. A ghost town from which even the ghosts had gone missing – leaving just an emptiness.

In the shadows, something moved.

The outline of a child was briefly visible, then it disappeared into the gloom again. It emerged from the shadows once more – a small girl, clutching a teddy bear, picking her way through the refrigeration pipes and valves. Then she was gone.

The ghost of a child.

The panicking customers found themselves in the Docking Bays, and they needed no further encouragement. They ran blindly for the nearest spacecraft they could find, pushing and fighting to get on board. Many mercenaries followed unthinkingly after them, then found themselves trapped when the air-lock hatches sealed shut. The Docking Bays were full of the sound of automatic voices intoning the undocking sequences.

'Pier 27 – switching to primary power . . .'

'Pier 9 – locking arms disengaged . . .'

'Pier 83 – switching to primary power . . .'

'Pier 106 – undocking sequence in progress . . .'

'Pier 27 – undocking sequence in progress . . .'

'Pier 52 – spacecraft ready to clear Iceworld . . .'

'Pier 8 – locking arms disengaged . . .'

'Pier 73 – switching to primary power . . .'

One by one, the tiny spacecraft began to drift clear of Iceworld's crystalline docking arms, free of the evil colony's icy clutch, and slowly out into the fresh darkness of space.

Stellar was beginning to feel frightened. She and Ted were lost in a huge ice chamber full of shadows. She picked her way carefully through the ice towards the light that was coming from behind one of the ice walls. Round another corner she found herself in a brightly lit clearing. Open vats steamed with a cold mist that fell to the ground and lay in a chill fog round Stellar's ankles. A large cabinet with a clear lid stood in the centre of the light, and Stellar could see a man lying inside. She was glad to meet someone else and she wondered if he was asleep, or if he was just resting.

A sudden hiss from the cabinet made her jump.

The clear lid began to swing open and a cold mist washed over the sides. Stellar watched apprehensively as the man inside slowly sat up. He turned to look at her. As soon as she saw his piercing black eyes, she knew that he wasn't going to help her. But for some reason she wasn't able to run away back into the shadows and hide. She couldn't take her eyes off his. She watched as he lowered his legs to the ground and stood up. She knew she wanted to run away, but she couldn't. She watched as he approached her. His eyes made her skin shiver. He looked at her.

Uncertainly, she held her teddy out. The man looked at it.

'Ted says he's sorry if he woke you up.'

The man looked up, into the dark shadows of the chamber. He was thinking of somewhere else, re-membering something that had happened a long time ago. He looked back at Stellar, then turned away, and strode out of the chamber.

Stellar hugged Ted close to her.

Glitz had grown more and more worried as he ran through the deserted Iceworld. The corridors were littered with things that people had dropped in their panic to escape, and Glitz knew that something terrible had happened. He raced to the Lower Docking Bays.

He couldn't believe what he saw. The piers should all have been full with berthed spacecraft, but instead the status boards all indicated empty. He raced to Pier 63.

As he ran, he noticed that just one or two piers still had spacecraft berthed, but the automatic voices softly marked the progress of their undocking sequences. If he had arrived at Pier 63 just a few moments earlier he would have been in time. But he didn't. He saw three huge mercenaries forcing the last remaining customers into the air-lock that led to the *Nosferatu*.

'Here, what's going on?' he shouted from across the Docking Bays. But the three mercenaries took no notice, and the air-lock door began to slide shut behind them.

'Stand clear of the door, please,' intoned the emotionless automatic voice.

Glitz threw himself towards the air-lock door, but it was already shut. 'What's the big idea? Open up!' He banged his fist uselessly against the steel door.

'Pier 63 – switching to primary power . . .'

'What's going on?' he cried with increasing desperation.

'Pier 63 – undocking sequence in progress . . .'

'You can't go without me!' Glitz turned to look out of the observation window.

Outside, the long arm of the air-lock, which reached from the Docking Bays to the spacecraft entrance hatch, was sliding back into the bay. Beyond, against the black sky, Glitz saw hundreds of spacecraft fleeing from Iceworld. He looked helplessly back to the *Nosferatu* and saw the locking arms, which held the spacecraft clamped securely in position, swinging clear of its hull.

'Pier 63 – locking arms disengaged . . .'

Glitz was desperate. 'No, there must be some mistake!' But he knew that there was nothing he could do to stop it.

'Pier 63 – spacecraft ready to clear Iceworld . . .'

Small manoeuvering rockets pushed the *Nosferatu* clear of the docking arm, and then began to thrust the spacecraft out into the dark night of space.

'Safe journey and good fortune, *Nosferatu* . . .' intoned the automatic voice, without feeling.

Glitz was heartbroken. Through the observation window, he watched his spacecraft slowly drifting away.

'No – you can't leave! Not after all these years. Come back! I should be coming with you.'

In his Control Room, Kane jabbed at a button. The shutter on his observation window slid back, and Kane looked at all the tiny spacecraft fleeing into the night. Terrified people trying to escape from him. A slight smile creased his face for a moment. This is what it would be like when he returned to Proamon. This is what it would be like throughout the Twelve Galaxies!

Glitz banged in grief on the Docking Bay observation window. 'Oy! Take me with you! Please . . .'

Kane looked at the hundreds of spacecraft, and thought of them full of innocent people and his force of frozen mercenaries. There must be no witnesses to the terror which was just starting. No cries of warning. No one must escape.

He pressed another button. The night sky was suddenly filled with the simultaneous burst of explosions.

Glitz didn't understand what had happened. He saw the huge blast that tore through the *Nosferatu* and blew it into fragments. He saw the explosions from the other spacecraft that burst in the sky like hundreds of fireworks. He knew that five hundred spacecraft had just blown up. But he didn't really understand what had happened. He didn't comprehend that two thousand lives had just ceased to exist. Two thousand lives had just been extinguished, like a beam of light being switched off. Two thousand tiny, insignificant lives, each one as precious as a diamond, had been scratched out like errors.

Glitz never really understood. But he felt the huge, black pain of it, all the same. He crumpled, and fell to his knees in grief.

Kane stood for several minutes, watching the fragments of wreckage sparkling against the black. Then he closed the observation window.

Glitz looked up. His face was hard. He knew who had done this.

'Kane!'

Like everywhere else in Iceworld, the Freezer Centre was deserted. Items of melting foodstuff were trampled into the floor, and small puddles of water collected round the bases of the freezer chests.

The Doctor hurried in, with Mel and Ace in tow. He didn't like the empty silence. 'Where is everyone?' he muttered darkly. 'Half-day closing? Some kind of fire drill? I don't think we have much time.'

He marched over to the TARDIS and fished the key out of his pocket. Ace was getting restless. She'd expected them to go straight to the Docking Bays.

'What are we doing here? I thought we was going to see your spacecraft?'

Mel smiled. 'This *is* our spacecraft.'

Ace looked at the tall blue cabinet which the Doctor was trying to unlock. Then she looked at Mel, laughing at Ace. She almost thumped Mel. 'I'm not stupid!' she said, trying to contain her anger.

The Doctor opened a narrow door, and disappeared inside. Ace couldn't work out what was going on. Mel smiled sympathetically at Ace and said, 'Believe me . . .' and then disappeared through the door too. Ace was amazed. She stood watching for a few moments, waiting for Mel and the Doctor to step back out of the cabinet. But instead she heard Mel's voice from inside: 'Come on. Come and see for yourself.'

'This is stupid,' said Ace. But she was curious to know what was so important inside this box. 'Squeeze up, then.'

She pushed her way into the box, expecting to be squashed up against Doughnut and the Professor inside. She looked around, startled. At first, she thought she'd made a mistake, and pushed through one of the Freezer

119

Centre exit doors accidentally. She was inside some kind of brightly lit control room, and the Doctor was flicking through star charts on a large viewing screen. But how had she got into the Doctor's spacecraft from the Freezer Centre? She turned back to look at the door she'd just come through. It was a large pair of double doors, not the small, narrow door she remembered walking through. Was her mind playing tricks? Had she fallen unconscious, or something? She stepped back to the doors, and looked out through them.

Outside the TARDIS, Ace's head popped out through the open door for a moment, looked around in amazement, and then disappeared again.

'Hang about . . .'

What was going on here? Were they playing some kind of a joke on her? Someone had some explaining to do, and Ace turned on Mel in annoyance. 'Here – how d'you do that?'

Mel had never really understood the technicalities of it herself, so she just shrugged her shoulders and smiled. 'It's bigger on the inside than it is on the outside.'

'Don't come all clever dick with me. What's going on?'

'It's difficult to explain.'

'Try me.'

'Well – it's dimensionally transcendental, you see.'

The Doctor, meanwhile, was studying a particular star chart, but with all this chatter in the background he could hardly think. '*Quiet!*' he bellowed.

Mel and Ace turned to look at the Doctor with slight surprise.

'That's better,' said the Doctor. 'Now, since the planet Proamon doesn't appear to exist, at least according to the TARDIS star charts, I think it's time we had a word with Mr Kane. Come on, there are things to do.' And he brushed past the two women and out into the Freezer Centre.

'Come on,' said Mel, leading Ace out.

While the Doctor was locking the TARDIS door, Ace peered round the back of the TARDIS, just to make sure it wasn't all some magician's illusion . . .

Glitz had returned to the chamber of the Singing Trees, and not finding the two women there, realised that they must have returned to Iceworld with the Doctor. At least, that's what he hoped had happened.

He was making his way back along the metal gantries in the upper Ice Passages, when he suddenly heard the heavy, ringing footsteps of several mercenaries from another passage. He looked back down the passage just in time to see them lurch out of a side passage, and turn towards him.

Nearly all of Kane's frozen mercenaries had been destroyed in the spacecraft, but evidently these half-dozen-or-so had escaped being trapped with the customers. Glitz took one look at them, and started to run. The Sprog had mentioned something about having a store of nitro back in her quarters. Glitz needed to borrow some . . .

McLuhan was taking most of Bazin's weight as they staggered down endless Ice Passages. Even if they managed to kill the alien creature now, there was no certainty that they would ever be able to find their way out of the Ice Passages again. But that was a problem that could wait. She kept glancing at the signal tracker, and had noticed that the Creature was pursuing them once more and was gaining on them. They would soon have to stand and fight. She didn't know whether the fight would come before or after their one hour fifty-three minutes were up.

Bazin was in considerable pain, and could hardly stand. 'Leave me. Leave me here . . .' he gasped.

'I'm not leaving you anywhere.'

'Don't be stupid. I'm slowing you down . . .'

'We're not in any hurry.'

'One hour fifty-three minutes . . .'

At first, McLuhan wasn't sure that she'd heard Bazin properly. 'What?'

'Average survival on an ANT-hunt: one hour fifty-three. We're way past that.'

'Who told you rubbish like that?' demanded McLuhan.

'Everyone knows it.'

'You stick to your rule book.'

'Like you, you mean?'

McLuhan looked at him. She was getting to like the boy. 'Yes, well, we can't all be perfect soldiers. Look – we'll take cover over there.' McLuhan had seen a small alcove in the Ice Passage, with a number of low boulders at the front. It was the best they'd find down here.

She hauled Bazin over the boulders, and lowered him to the ground. Then she kneeled down, and unclamped her Cosmolite. She set the gun up pointing between two boulders, and took cover in the alcove with Bazin. 'Here,' she said, handing him the signal tracker. 'I can't line the gun up and read the tracker at the same time. You'll have to read the signal.' She lay down flat on her stomach, and adjusted herself to the Cosmolite. 'This ANT won't be able to tell its toes from its tentacles when I've finished with it.' She flicked up the gunsight, and then settled her finger on the trigger. 'Right – where is it?'

Bazin was watching the signal tracker. It was following the radio signal from the map, still tucked into the Creature's folds of skin where the Doctor had left it. 'About two hundred metres away. Approaching from the left.'

McLuhan lined her sights up on the passage to the far left. All she had to do now was wait for the ANT to walk into the centre of the sights . . .

Glitz clambered up a service shaft leading from the Ice

Passages to the basement areas of Iceworld. He had just reached the top, when a strident voice pierced the air. 'Ah – you there!'

Glitz froze in surprise and terror.

'Yes – you. Where is everyone? What kind of a way is this to run a business?'

Glitz turned round to see a white sparkly thing festooned in fluffy pink feathers bearing down on him.

'Have you seen a small child anywhere? She answers to the name of Stellar. I appear to have mislaid her.'

Glitz was lost for words.

The woman peered at him, but quickly decided from the man's vacuous expression that he was a complete buffoon. 'Evidently not. Well, if you find her, would you be so good as to take her to the Refreshment Bar to wait for me?'

The woman turned to leave, but then turned back again and looked at Glitz. 'Don't just stand there gawking, man. Start looking for her.'

'Certainly, missus.'

Glitz turned a little confusedly, and started looking, while the woman flounced off in a quiver of pink ostrich. Glitz had already peered uncertainly behind two fire extinguishers and an ash tray before he realised what he was doing ...

The Doctor was hurrying through the empty corridors.

'Ask him what he's up to,' Ace kept insisting, as the two women hurried along in the Doctor's tracks. But Mel knew better than to pester the Doctor with trivial questions when he was in this kind of a mood.

Suddenly, Ace halted, and pointed at an access ladder on the wall that led down to the floors below. 'Here – this is a short cut to my quarters. It's right underneath us. Look.'

Mel looked at the ladder. There was some graffiti felt-tipped onto the wall beside it:

ACE 4 WAYNE

'Ace for Wayne?' said Mel with a slight smile.

'Yeah, he's my stuffed dog.' Then Ace realised what Mel had been thinking, and turned on Mel accusingly. 'Here, who d'you think he was?'

'Come on, you two!' called the Doctor from down the corridor. 'Why are you always squabbling?'

'Come on,' said Mel.

'No – wait. I just want to pop back to my quarters. I feel a bit naked without a couple of cans of nitro.'

'There isn't time.'

'Will you two hurry up!'

'I'll only be a sec.' Ace was already half-way down the ladder. 'I'll catch you up before you reach Kane's Cryogenics Chamber.' And she was gone.

Mel ran and caught up with the Doctor. 'What's happened to Ace?' he asked in concern.

'She's gone back to her quarters. But she said not to wait for her.'

The Doctor was annoyed by this time-wasting. 'I'll have something to say to her when I see her again. Come on. The Creature's still in danger.'

'I hope it's found somewhere to hide. Somewhere safe . . .'

McLuhan was calm as she lay with her finger pulling gently on the Cosmolite's trigger. She heard the quiet ticking of the signal tracker that Bazin was holding.

'One hundred metres,' he said, as the ticking grew slightly faster.

For some reason, an incident from her childhood suddenly came into McLuhan's mind. She and her gang of friends had been playing in a disused quarry, and the boys had dared the girls to climb up a rock face. There were plenty of hand- and footholds, but it was almost vertical. The smallest girl had got halfway up, then got frightened. McLuhan was nearest to her and had started to edge towards the small girl. She kept looking at her and could see the sheer terror in the small girl's eyes. But before McLuhan could reach her, the expression in the girl's eyes changed. It was almost as if the small girl had realised that the choice between life and death was hers, and had decided to fall. Even as a child, McLuhan knew at that moment that the other girl would fall before she could reach her.

'Fifty metres. It's there!' Bazin's voice brought her back to the Ice Passages.

She saw the ANT appear at the edge of her gunsight, moving towards the cross-wires in the centre, and she pulled her finger another millimetre further back, until she felt the resistance of the trigger point.

She knew what she had to do. She saw it all clearly now – a simple choice between black and white. All the inessential greys of everyday life had melted away: all the half-truths and half-lies that everyone tells; all the confused emotions and confused relationships that everyone lives through; all the delayed decisions and delayed affection that no one ever finds time for. All were now reduced to a simple black and white for McLuhan – either live or die; win or lose; kill or be killed. A simple choice. A simple morality. A simple outcome. She saw it all clearly now, and she liked it better this way.

The gunsight's cross-wires bisected the Creature horizontally and vertically. McLuhan pulled back another millimetre on the trigger. She felt the Cosmolite kick slightly against her shoulder, and she saw through the gunsight as the .65 gigawatt bolt-beam blew the Creature apart.

CHAPTER FOURTEEN

Ace keyed in the security number of her door, and disappeared inside. She looked round the room and identified a small hold-all underneath the mess. She fished it out, and then retrieved a rather shapeless stuffed dog from one end of the bed. She smiled at Wayne, pushing him into the hold-all. She turned to the racks of chemistry equipment, inspecting the contents of one or two flasks, but shook her head.

Suddenly she froze. There was a noise behind her – the slight creaking of a door. She hardly dared turn to look.

She inched slowly round.

She gave a huge sigh of relief when she saw what had given her such a fright. She hadn't closed the door of the fridge properly, and it was swinging slightly ajar. It was a tall fridge-freezer, and the door creaked on its hinges. She pushed the door closed.

A gloved hand suddenly appeared from inside the fridge and jammed the door open.

Ace's heart missed a beat.

Kane pushed the door wide open, and stepped out. 'You're so predictable . . .'

Ace backed away from him. 'I'm not frightened of you.' But Kane's eyes saw right through her lie.

'You can kill me – I still won't come and work for you.'

'Possibly not – although I think you overestimate your

capacity to withstand pain. I can cause pain in ways that you can't even imagine.' He began to advance on Ace. 'But all this would take time. And I can't wait for that. My pleasure will have to be postponed for a while. There are much faster ways of obtaining the assistance I require.'

He grabbed at Ace's arm, and twisted it violently behind her back. She gasped out in pain.

There was terror on her face, as Kane shoved her roughly through the door.

The Creature seemed brittle and flimsy, lying dead in the snow. McLuhan almost felt sorry for it. She saw that it was a bio-mechanoid – part living creature, part android. The two halves of its structure were now mixed up – splintered bones with fractured steel rods, torn flesh with burst polythene tubing – but she marvelled at the intricacy and ingenuity of its manufacture. The fusion of organic and mechanical engineering.

She also saw that Bazin was weak, and needed medical treatment immediately. 'Come on – its head. Then we're finished.' She unclipped a small laser knife from her belt, and started to burn through the neck of the Creature.

'Can't we just leave the head?'

'Mr Kane wants the head. And I'm not leaving the job half-finished, even if I do have to cut an ANT's head off.'

'What does he want the head for, anyway?'

'Not our job to ask questions. Maybe he wants it stuffed, on the wall. There, that should do it.' She put the laser knife down, and began to pull at the Creature's head. As she pulled, the membrane sheath covering the head began to tear. McLuhan's face screwed in disgust as she felt the mucus-covered skull beneath the sheath. She pulled harder, twisting the head as she did so, and the outer sheath tore completely. The sections of the skull fell away in McLuhan's hands, and she instinctively dropped it to the ground.

The skull cracked apart, and for a moment, McLuhan and Bazin could see the fabulous crystal, crackling with the electric storm trapped inside it. The contacts holding the crystal in place fractured, and then shattered completely. It seemed as if a seal had been broken, allowing the fire inside to flow out. The air surrounding the crystal flashed and sparked, as twisting streaks of energy forked out from the crystal.

'The Dragon's Treasure!' whispered McLuhan, entranced by the awesome beauty of it. Bazin was so hypnotised by the crystal that he no longer felt any pain from his injury.

The electric fingers continued to dance in the air, reaching further and further out from the crystal. McLuhan realised that the flickering storm was getting dangerous. 'Let's get out of here!'

But the tongues of fire surged outwards, and began to lick at the bodies of McLuhan and Bazin. The two guards felt the stabbing pain, and turned to run, but the twisting sparks wrapped themselves round the two bodies. The two guards tried to fight free, but the crystal had found its victims.

A violent surge of energy shot through the crackling web that entangled the two guards, and galvanised their bodies. The jolt threw their heads backwards, and they felt a momentary, searing pain flashing through every nerve fibre in their body. Then they were dead. The crackling storm began to subside and retreat back into the crystal.

Soon there was nothing to be seen except three bodies in the snow and a large crystal that glittered with a fire twisting inside it.

Glitz knew the way to Ace's quarters, but he was surprised to find her door open.

'Sprog?' he whispered cautiously, entering the room. 'Ace?'

He looked round. He didn't know whether anything was wrong or not – the place always looked a mess. He closed the door behind him.

He didn't have much time, so he hurried. He wanted all the explosive he could lay his hands on, along with any detonators, and about fifty metres of fine wire. There was a hold-all on the bed, which he started filling with the aerosol cans that had *Nitro – Fingers Off!* felt-tipped on them. There were about a dozen of them altogether. Then he started rummaging through the cupboards. He soon found the one with all Ace's experimental gear in it.

The detonators were in a box marked *Big Bang Explosives Co. – Blue Nitroglycerin – Danger!* It was a pity Ace hadn't kept the original contents of the box. Glitz read the manufacturer's warning:

1. *Do not expose to sunlight.*
2. *Do not drop.*
3. *Do not shake.*
4. *Do not place on a wobbly table.*
5. *Do not store indoors.*
6. *Do not store within 2,000 metres of inhabited buildings.*
7. *Please dispose of used sticks tidily.*

Big Bang Explosives Co.

Where in heavens had the Sprog managed to get hold of blue nitroglycerin? And what had she used it for!

Glitz emptied the detonators into the hold-all and threw the empty box away. He grabbed a long reel of small-gauge wire, and dropped that in the bag as well, then looked round to see if he'd missed anything.

He carefully picked up the hold-all, and opened the door. Those deep-frozen mercenaries weren't going to know their toes from their tentacles by the time he'd finished with them!

Mel had to lead the way towards the Cryogenics Chamber, because the Doctor had never been there. She had to detour down through the Ice Passages so that she could retrace the route she and Ace had taken when they were running away from Kane. They hurried through the snow.

Suddenly, they saw the Creature.

Mel stopped dead, not daring to believe what she saw. The Creature's mutilated body was lying dead in the snow. Beyond were the bodies of two guards. Fallen between them, the crystal was glowing gently.

'The Creature! It's dead. They've killed it!'

Mel was too upset even to cry. She knelt beside the Creature, and reached out to touch its gossamer-soft body.

The Doctor went over to the two dead guards, and turned them over. 'But it had a final surprise for anyone who might interfere with it – a huge energy surge when the crystal was disconnected.' He looked at the two guards. 'Poor fools.'

Mel looked up at him. 'How can you feel sorry for them? They killed the Creature!'

'I feel sorry for all death, no matter how wrong the people were. *Every* life is precious.' He let the bodies fall back, and turned to Mel and the Creature.

Mel looked down. 'What shall we do now? It's too late to save the Creature.'

'We'll try to finish its work for it – and put an end to all this evil and death.' Carefully, he lifted the crystal out of the snow, and passed it to Mel. 'This is what everyone has died for. It's time the dying ended . . .'

'Target temperature achieved. Ambient cabinet temperature: minus 193 °C.'

Stellar jumped as the seals on the cabinet hissed open, and the lid gently rose. The refrigerating gases washed over the sides, and Stellar looked at Ted lying inside, with a light sparkling of frost on his fur. She smiled, and reached out to pick him up. But she knew something was wrong, even before she touched him. She could feel the icy cold surrounding him, and she pulled her hand back.

She knew that it would hurt if she touched him, so she looked round for something to pick him up with. There were some rags lying on the floor in a corner, along with a few workman's tools. She took the rags, and folded them until they were several layers thick. Then she wrapped them round Ted's leg, and lifted him out of the cabinet. But even through the thickness of the rags, she could feel the cold beginning to bite, and she dropped the toy.

It hit the ice floor, and shattered like a glass ornament.

'Ted!'

The small girl didn't move. She just looked down at the splinters on the ground. Ted was everything to her. He'd been with her since she was a baby. They'd had adventures together, travelled through the galaxies together, and grown up together. She hadn't wanted to hurt him. She'd thought he wanted to go in the cabinet – like the man.

Stellar knelt down, and reached to touch the tiny pieces. Her eyes were beginning to fill with tears. 'I'm sorry, Ted. I didn't know.'

The tears trickled down her cheeks, and fell in small droplets. They turned into tiny crystals of ice before they touched the ground.

'I'm sorry, Ted...' she sobbed.

It was a bit primitive, but it would have the desired effect. Glitz stood back and surveyed his handiwork. Fine wires criss-crossed round the perimeter of the Cryogenics Chamber at knee height. If you looked carefully, you could see that each one was connected to a detonator embedded in a small lump of plastic nitro. Glitz hoped that the wires themselves weren't too noticeable.

He tightened a couple of the wires, then sat down in the middle of the chamber. All he had to do now was wait

131

for Kane's frosted thugs to come and find him!

Mel and the Doctor were hurrying silently through the corridors of Iceworld with the Dragonfire crystal, when Mel heard a familiar sound. From the other end of the corridor came the measured footfall of the small band of mercenaries, accidentally left alive after Kane destroyed all the spacecraft.

'What is it?' asked the Doctor suspiciously. But Mel didn't have time to reply before the dead-faced killers swung round the corner, and started to bear down on them.

'This way, Doctor!' cried Mel, darting down another corridor. The Doctor hurried after her.

Glitz was startled to look up and see Mel burst into the Cryogenics Chamber.

'Glitz!' she exclaimed, and hurried towards him.

'*Stop!*' cried Glitz in alarm.

Mel froze, and looked round uncertainly. 'What's the matter?'

'I think it might have something to do with that trip-wire you almost walked through,' observed the Doctor, catching up with her. Mel looked down. Her leg was right up against one of the wires.

'Carefully, now,' cautioned Glitz, as Mel hitched her skirt up, and gingerly climbed over the wire.

'They're right behind us, Glitz!'

'Come on, Doctor – you too. We'll be all right on the inside. How many of them are there?'

'About ten.'

Glitz looked round. 'Well, we should have just enough to deal with them. Hurry up! And keep as close to the middle as you can, away from the edges.' Glitz heard the leaden tread of the mercenaries, approaching down the corridor, and as he retreated to the centre of the chamber, the leading mercenary stumbled through the entrance. It was followed by the others. They stood in the entrance for a moment, trying to identify their victims in the gloom.

Glitz stared at them. 'Been sent by Kane, have you?' he shouted. 'Well, I've got a message for your proprietor!'

The mercenaries began to stagger towards Glitz. 'That's it,' he taunted. 'Come over here, where I can whisper it in your orifices.'

The mercenaries were circling Glitz, as he'd hoped, and the leading killer was approaching one of the trip-wires.

'Come on, you Neanderthal maggot-brains! Let's see what you're made of!'

The leading mercenary strode forward, and broke the wire.

Nothing happened.

Glitz looked in horror. The ice-cold murderer continued to advance on Glitz.

'No, stay back. Keep away.' Glitz began to back away nervously. 'No, just a joke ...'

To the left, a huge explosion brought down one of the following mercenaries, as it snapped a different wire. A series of explosions ripped round the perimeter of the chamber, when the other mercenaries also began to close in. But the leading mercenary was still advancing on Glitz and the others.

Glitz looked round quickly. All the other mercenaries were now lying dead on the ground. There was just this one still alive. 'Run for it!' shouted Glitz to the Doctor and Mel. 'I'll keep this one busy while you get out!' He grabbed at the empty hold-all which was lying on the ground, and threw it at the mercenary. The mercenary didn't even blink.

'No, Glitz – we're staying here with you!' called the Doctor.

'Don't be stupid!' shouted Glitz, throwing the empty

reel of wire, which bounced off the mercenary's chest. 'There's no reason why we should *all* be killed.' He grabbed at the stuffed animal which Ace had left in the hold-all, and hurled it desperately.

The stuffing in Wayne, the nondescript stuffed dog, consisted of 60% polyester, 28% nylon, 8% linen, 4% cotton, a small amount of fireproofing residue, and two dead moths. And three sticks of blue nitroglycerin...

The explosion blew Glitz, the Doctor and Mel ten metres across the floor. The cryogenics tubes within fifteen metres all shattered from the force of the blast. And a section of the roofing girder immediately above came crashing down.

Ace!

Glitz, the Doctor and Mel dragged themselves off the floor, and looked round. Glitz picked one of Wayne's ears off the floor – it was all that was left of the unremarkable stuffed dog.

'I might have known that anything belonging to Sprog was liable to explode on impact...' he muttered.

The Doctor was also talking to himself, as he looked at bodies of the dead mercenaries, 'More death. I suppose they were already dead inside, but it's so senseless.'

It took Mel, still clutching the glowing crystal, to ask the single really important question: 'Where's Ace?'

They all looked at each other. 'Isn't she here?' asked the Doctor. 'Glitz – hasn't Ace got here yet?

'I thought she was with you two.'

Almost as if in reply to Mel's question, Iceworld's public address system hummed into life, and Kane's voice drifted through the deserted corridors: 'Doctor... Glitz... I know you can hear me.'

Kane held the struggling Ace tight, as he spoke into the microphone. He knew that the Doctor and Glitz would be listening somewhere to what he said. 'I'd like to propose a transaction. My very final transaction before I leave Svartos for ever. The Dragonfire for the girl. Bring me the Dragonfire, and you can have the girl. A special Closing-Down Sale, you might call it. But hurry – while stocks last.'

He looked at Ace with an evil smile, and jabbed at the intercom button.

In the Cryogenics Chamber, the loudspeakers went dead. The Doctor, Mel and Glitz were looking at each other.

'He means it, Doctor,' warned Glitz.

'I've no doubt.'

'But we can't give him the treasure,' pleaded Mel.

The Doctor looked grim. 'We don't have any choice. The Creature is already dead. Ace is still alive ...'

CHAPTER FIFTEEN

Kane's eyes blazed triumphantly. 'At last...' he whispered. 'After three thousand years... Bring it closer.'

Mel took a small step towards Kane. She looked at Ace who was still held tight by Kane and obviously frightened.

The Doctor had been watching Kane's eyes, trying to get the measure of his match, and he decided that the cheery approach would be most effective. 'Three thousand years, eh? That's long enough for an entire civilisation to have come and gone.'

Kane turned to inspect the oddly-dressed man who was smiling affably. 'Are you some kind of an idiot?' he asked slowly.

The Doctor strode forward, beaming, and extended a hand. 'I'm the Doctor. These two are my friends Mel and Glitz. And the small one that you're holding in a menacing fashion is Ace.'

Kane knew he was being made a fool of. His expression twisted angrily as he tightened his grip on Ace.

'Doctor!' screamed Ace, in fear.

The Doctor halted. 'Ah. You know, for someone who's had the patience to wait three thousand years, you seem to be in rather a hurry suddenly.'

'Here,' broke in Glitz, 'what's all this three thousand years?'

The Doctor looked at Kane. 'Three thousand years since you were exiled here from Proamon – along with the Creature.'

Kane's piercing gaze tried to read the Doctor. 'Who *are* you?'

'Oh, just a traveller.'

'What do you know of Proamon?' Kane turned his eyes on the others.

'The Creature showed us everything,' said Mel, 'on the hologram.'

For a moment, Kane looked away, thinking of something else. 'The archives . . . I was going to destroy them.'

'Oh, keep them for the souvenir value,' suggested the Doctor, 'along with the Ice Garden.'

'But why was the Creature doing time here as well?' asked Glitz.

Kane turned angrily on him. 'The bio-mechanoid was my *jailer*! Look around. Controls lying dead. Power units waiting for an energy source . . . The Dragonfire is the energy source!'

At last, the Doctor was beginning to understand. 'And without the crystal's energy, you were powerless.'

'My people thought they could imprison me on this wretched planet by implanting the power source inside the Creature. They shall learn of their folly.'

'A living creature was created as the key to your prison! Fascinating.'

Kane's eyes drifted away again – drifted back over three thousand years. 'There were times when I ached for death – to journey from the cold, dark face of Svartos, round to the sun-blistered surface on the other side, where I would quickly die. But I was owed my revenge!' Kane's eyes blazed with anger once more. 'And now, with the Dragonfire, I have the power to return to Proamon and exact my revenge!' He nodded at Mel, who was holding the crystal. 'The girl – you – bring me the

Dragonfire!'

Mel clutched the crystal tighter. 'No! I'm not going to lift one finger to help you.'

Ace panicked. 'Melanie!' she cried, and turned to plead with Kane. 'Don't listen to her. She doesn't mean it.' She turned back to Mel, begging her, 'Doughnut! Give him the treasure, please. I'm only sixteen. I'm too young to be freeze-dried!'

'Come on, Mel,' joined in Glitz. 'This isn't the time for being fastidious.'

Mel didn't know who to listen to. If she gave the crystal to Kane, he would use its power for evil. If she didn't, he would kill Ace. She turned to the Doctor for help. 'Doctor?'

The Doctor tried to play for more time with Kane. 'If I could just explain . . .' But Kane snatched off one of his gloves, and held his bare hand towards Ace.

Ace screamed in terror: 'Doctor!'

'Stop wasting my time,' hissed Kane. 'The Dragonfire is mine now. Either you can give it to me willingly, or I shall take it from your dead bodies.'

The Doctor turned helplessly to Mel. 'The logic is inescapable.' Defeated, Mel stepped slowly forward with the crystal.

Kane smiled in triumph. 'Place it in the circuit – there.' He indicated a crystalline structure in the centre of the room. The Dragonfire fitted neatly into a gap. 'Now – away!'

Mel stepped back again. Kane pressed a sequence of buttons on the Control Desk. The crystalline structure began to close round the Dragonfire. As it locked into position, the immense fire was released from the Dragonfire once more. But this time, instead of twisting in empty air, the optical energy was focused by the array of crystals surrounding it, and concentrated into a powerful beam that burned upwards to another crystalline structure suspended above it. This split the beam into hundreds of tiny, focused rays of light, which reflected and refracted throughout the crystalline structure of the Control Room.

As the energy circulated rapidly round the Control Room, empty screens and monitors flickered back into life. The whole room seemed to be waking from a deep sleep. Kane released Ace to concentrate on the newly activated controls. She ran to Mel's arms.

Kane punched control switches and keyed in instrument settings, and slowly the whole room began to vibrate.

Mel held onto Ace. 'Doctor, – what's happening?'

The Doctor listened to the growing roar in amazement. 'It sounds like a starflight photon drive.'

'Starflight drive?' echoed Glitz. 'It can't be . . .'

The huge crystalline limbs, towering over the shadows on the dark side of the planet Svartos, began to move and crack. Huge beams of ice snapped under the strain, and crashed down. Slowly, the immense structure began to rise out of the planet's surface, shaking off its chains of confinement. From beneath the planet's surface, more crystalline limbs broke free, and as it drifted clear of the planet, it looked like a colossal snow crystal, floating away into space.

'This is a spacecraft!' exclaimed Glitz. 'The whole colony's a spacecraft!'

As the giant snow crystal floated free of the planet's shadow, and out into the fierce sunlight, the ice began to melt, and the metallic structure of a spacecraft became visible under the centuries-old encrusted ice.

Kane looked around. The scanners and displays glowed obediently, waiting for his instructions. 'My hour of vengeance . . . I feel it!'

'Vengeance on whom?' intruded the Doctor. 'You're too late, Kane.'

'All your frozen mercenaries are dead now,' declared Mel.

Kane laughed. 'I can soon find more.'

'But where can you find another home planet?' insisted the Doctor.

'You're talking in riddles, Doctor. Proamon is my home planet – as you already know.'

'*Was* your home planet.'

Kane looked blankly at the Doctor.

'Check your navigational equipment,' insisted the Doctor. 'It's all fully operative now.'

Kane turned to the navigational guidance console and keyed in a set of co-ordinates. The screen responded with a star chart. Kane looked at the display, and then re-keyed the co-ordinates. 'There must be something wrong with it. A minor malfunction after three thousand years inactive...' He tried to correct the problem.

'Sadly not,' explained the Doctor. 'Your planet, your race, your entire civilisation were destroyed, one thousand years after you were exiled.'

'It's not possible...' Frantically, Kane punched at buttons, trying to correct the display.

'Look at the sun of Proamon. When you left, it was a cold Red Giant, surrounded by freezing planets.'

Kane looked. 'There's nothing here but a Neutron Star...'

'That's right. Your sun turned supernova two thousand years ago. All of its planets were engulfed in the explosion. Your people were annihilated. Your planet was obliterated. You're too late for your revenge, Kane.'

'My home...'

'A civilisation at its height, and suddenly – nothing.' The Doctor turned to Kane. He saw the terrible realisation on Kane's face, and suddenly felt sorry for him. 'You have no home.'

'No! No!' Kane's voice hardened again. He spun round, and punched furiously at a button. 'No! It shall not be!'

'No! Don't do that!' cried the Doctor.

The shutter covering the observation window began to slide open. The blinding bright sunlight streamed through the widening gap. An impersonal automatic voice intoned a warning: 'Danger. Unfiltered sunlight.'

'Get down, everyone!' shouted the Doctor. 'Take cover!' The others dived behind the control consoles, and the Doctor threw himself after them. Kane didn't move. He watched, as the shutter opened wide, then he stepped into the burning light.

He felt his skin scorching. The searing heat of the sunlight burned into his flesh. His skin began to vaporise in the heat, and steam rose from his body. He opened his mouth wide and screamed in agony.

As his flesh melted away, his body began to shrink. He sank to the ground, twisting and screaming with the blinding pain.

Finally, the screams died away.

The Doctor reached round the front of the Control Desk with his brolly and knocked the button controlling the observation window. The shutter began to slide shut. Soon, the Control Room was safe again. The Doctor and the others emerged from hiding and looked round. All that was left of Kane was his insulating uniform. His body had melted completely away . . .

CHAPTER SIXTEEN

In the TARDIS Console Room, the Doctor was busy checking the stabiliser settings at the control console. Mel watched him. She liked this new incarnation. He was still a bit grumpy at times, and occasionally he behaved like a fool, but he cared deeply about people – *all* people, not just his friends.

'Well, I suppose it's time,' she said.

The Doctor was preoccupied with the TARDIS's controls. 'Yes – strange business, "time". It delights in frustrating our plans. All Kane's hatred and bitterness, thwarted by a quirk of time.'

'I meant, I suppose it's time I should be leaving...'

The Doctor looked up. His bright expression had dropped. 'Already?'

He looked so helpless, all of a sudden – like a child who'd lost his playmate. Mel tried to explain. 'I don't belong here. I'm not a traveller, like you. I need somewhere I feel I can belong...'

'But so soon?'

'It's time.' She smiled warmly, and reached to hug the Doctor, but he turned quickly away.

'Ah, yes – "time" again. Always keeps popping up when you least expect it! Just when you think there's no time left, suddenly you've got all the time in the universe, and there's a lot of time in the universe, believe me.'

For a moment, Mel saw something in the Doctor she'd never seen before – the lonely traveller, journeying to the ends of time in a battered blue Police Box, on a voyage with no start and no finish.

He turned to her. 'Think of me when you hear a clock strike...'

She embraced the Doctor warmly, and he hugged her.

Glitz coughed loudly as he strode into the TARDIS. 'Well, we've officially renamed this craft the *Nosferatu II*, and the engines are nicely warmed up – so, next stop sunny Perivale, eh Sprog?'

'S'pose so,' said Ace miserably, following Glitz into the TARDIS.

Mel turned to Glitz. 'Have you got room for another one?'

'You Perivale-bound as well?' asked Glitz in surprise.

'I was hoping you might take me a bit further.' She smiled ingratiatingly.

Glitz was getting suspicious. 'How *much* further?'

'How much further are you going?'

'Here – half a millisecond...'

'Excellent!' interrupted the Doctor. 'Mel can keep you out of mischief, Glitz.'

'And that means no more dodgy deals,' warned Mel.

'Thanks a billion, Doctor.' Glitz glared at the Doctor as they shook hands farewell. 'Well, come on then. You two can toss a coin to decide which of you has to scrape the ice off the windscreen...'

Mel turned quickly to the Doctor. 'Ace doesn't have anywhere to go, Doctor...' she whispered.

'Nonsense,' replied the Doctor. 'It's an idyllic place, Perivale. Lush green meadows... village blacksmith...'

'Doctor – she comes from the twentieth century!'

'Ah.'

'Come on, Mel,' called Glitz from the doorway. 'Get your digit out!'

Mel turned to leave. She looked back at the Doctor. 'I'll send you a postcard,' she promised.

'But I don't have an address.'

'I'll put it in a bottle, and throw it into space. It'll reach you – in time.'

Glitz and Mel left, and Ace trudged after them.

'Excuse me,' called the Doctor. 'Where do you think you're going?'

Ace looked back. 'Perivale.'

The Doctor's eyes twinkled. 'Ah, but which route are you taking? The direct route with Glitz – or the scenic route?'

Ace didn't know what to say. She could hardly believe this was true.

'Well, do you fancy a quick spin round the Twelve Galaxies, en route to Perivale?'

The girl from Perivale punched the air in delight. '*Ace!!*'

The Doctor tried to be stern. 'There are three rules. First: I'm in charge.'

'Anything you say, Professor!' agreed Ace, still bouncing with delight.

'Second: I'm not a Professor – I'm the Doctor.'

'Whatever you want!'

'And third...' The Doctor broke into a smile. 'Well... I'll think of a third one before we reach Perivale!'

Stellar had heard voices in the Freezer Centre, but when she got there, it was empty. She looked at the tall blue box which had appeared so mysteriously out of nowhere.

'*There* you are...' called her mother, from the other end of the Freezer Centre. 'I've been looking all over for you. Hurry up – we're late.' Her mother disappeared through an exit. Stellar ran after her. Then she stopped. There was a strange mechanical grinding sound coming from somewhere. She turned to look back at the tall blue box. There was nothing there now except a sort of blue flashing. She reached out, trying to catch the dancing blue light – but it receded quickly into the past, and disappeared.

The Starchild smiled. On a distant planet, the sun was rising on a new day.